I0827371

LAST TIME DOWN BLACKWATER

by

Sharon Decker

Library of Congress Cataloging-in-Publication Data

Last Time Down Blackwater, Sharon Decker

Summary: A collection of short stories about ordinary people who live in Flora-Bama, people who know nothing of antebellum mansions or mint juleps and whose lives are no walk on the beach.

ISBN: 978-1-939282-61-3

Published by Miniver Press, LLC, McLean Virginia

Previously published:

"Choctawhatchee," Alaska Quarterly

"Better By Now," South Dakota Review

"Somebody Needing Water," Cimarron Review

"Roses," Writers' Forum

"Dottie's Life," South Carolina Review

"The Soybean Field," West Branch

"Last Time Down Blackwater," Passages North

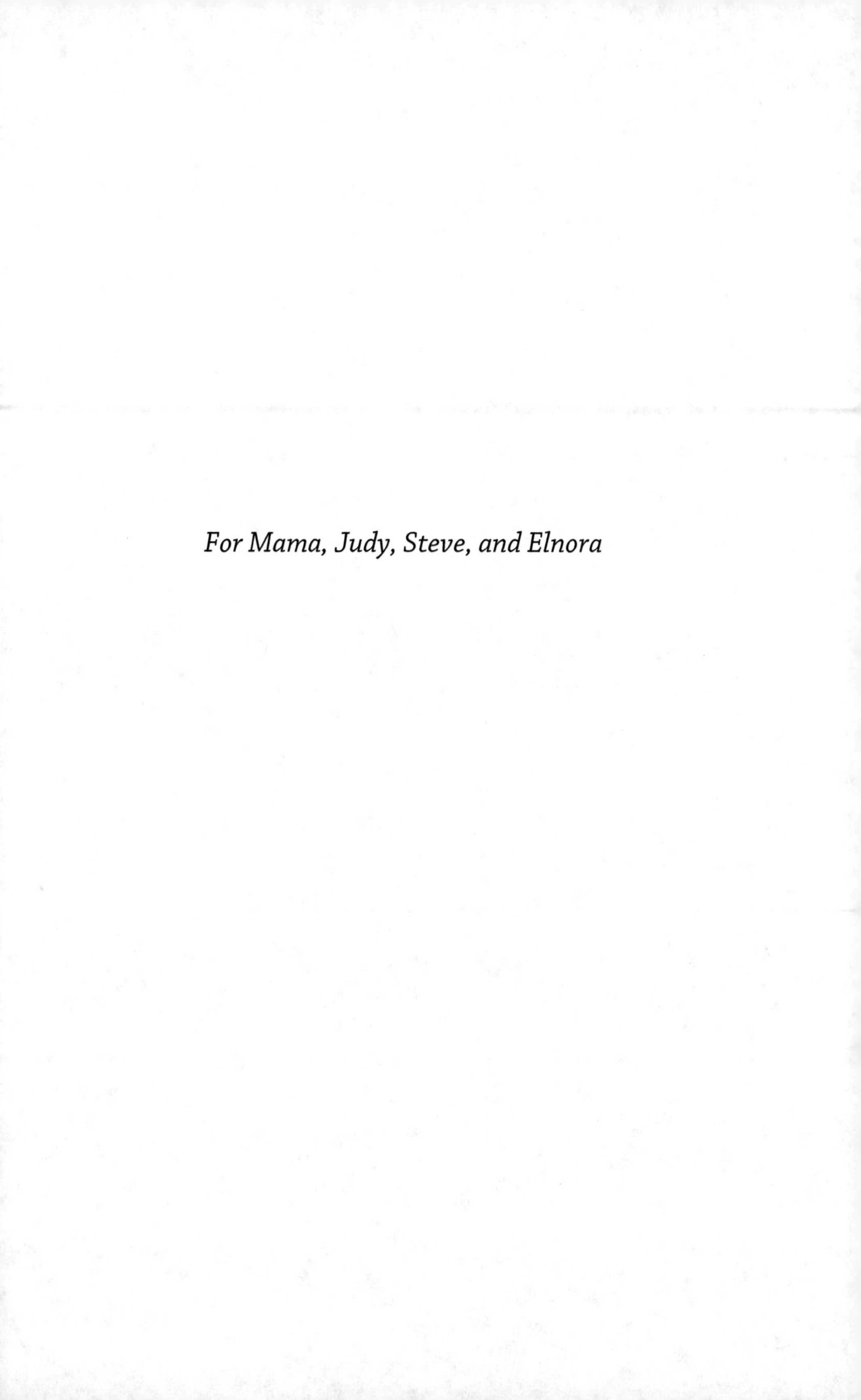

For Mama, Judy, Steve, and Elnora

TABLE OF CONTENTS

PREFACE

Flora-Bama is more than a famed, mullet-tossing honky-tonk at the edge of the Gulf of Mexico. It is a region. A region that straddles the state lines beyond the gleaming white sands of Destin, Florida, to Orange Beach on the 'Bama side, but it also stretches north, north to a land where pickup trucks fly down dusty, pine-shadowed back roads, the smell of fried chicken floats from cafes, and the humidity sticks with you like a hangover. It's a place where people still hold the door and ask how your mama's doing.

There are affluent folks in Flora-Bama, and at the opposite end are those who won't hit a lick at a snake, as my granny used to say. But most are average people: proud, bighearted, and true to their word. These are my people, and the following stories are about them and the ways they play the hand life deals them, for better or worse, like everyone everywhere.

The great migration to Florida is diluting the culture like ice melting in sweet tea—especially the closer you get to the beaches, where there has always been a mixture of the military, tourists, and those who move from elsewhere, as well as the locals. But you can bet there are still places where people stop their cars to let a funeral procession go by, and where, unless you behave in such a way as to "warrant" otherwise, you'll be treated with manners and respect.

CHOCTAWHATCHEE

Jesse is lying on our old plaid couch with his mama's Bible on his chest, watching TV. It's Sunday morning and the preachers are on, something he never misses now that he's sick, although the only time he ever mentioned God before he got emphysema was when he was cussing. I don't recognize the preacher he's watching, but he looks like all the rest to me, with his plasticky hair and his eyes popping out of his head. He's worked himself into a tizzy, which is what Jesse likes best. He likes that nearly as good as he likes the wrestling.

I stare out the window while I wash his plate and the pan I fried the eggs in, at the Choctawhatchee rolling past the bottom of the slope that is our backyard. It slides by like a big muddy snake, cypress hulls rising out of it like gnarled old men. For fifty-two years I've watched it go by, ever since Jesse brought me here to where he was raised. It's up right now, but not by much—not like it can be, swallowing the yard like it did in 1977 when it rained five days straight, the heaviest rain I ever saw, and turtles were paddling around the back porch and cottonmouths were crawling into my hydrangeas.

The TV is so loud I don't know how Rita can sleep back there, but then she always could sleep through a hurricane, ever since she was a baby. And she could always sleep as late as I let her, too, which was one reason she hated school so much and why she complained about it from the first day

I put her on the bus in the red corduroy dress I made and the patent leather shoes I shined with a biscuit, until the tenth grade when she got pregnant and quit.

My eggs and grits are still on the table, cold as a wedge, but I don't have an appetite for them this morning. It seems like I've eaten eggs and grits for a century now, and I'm just plain sick of them, and besides, my stomach is fluttering, the way it has been since she got here a week ago. It's the third time in three years that she's come to stay with us, and the last time she stayed six months.

Jesse griped all the way to the bus station. "She'll mess around and lose this one, too. You watch and see if she don't," he said, pulling into a gas station.

"She says he's not good to her."

"Yeah, that's the way she tells it, but he seemed nice enough to me, nicer by far than that last one. It's always something with that girl." He slammed the truck door, pumped the gas and got back in, gasping for air. "How many husbands is she going to go through anyhow? Fifty-one ain't no spring chicken, Norma. Hell, you and me had been married for a hundred years by then."

He gunned the engine and pulled right smack into the middle of a funeral procession. The people in the big white car ahead of us turned and stared.

"What the hell are y'all gawking at?" Jesse said, blowing the horn.

"It's a funeral!" I said, holding my hand over my eyes. I felt like crawling into the floorboard.

He jerked his foot off the gas pedal. "Oh. I didn't know that."

Now, Rita walks in, tying on a red robe.

"Morning," I say.

"Well, she's alive. Knock a block out from under the house," Jesse says, and every muscle in my neck and shoulders tenses up.

"I wouldn't be too sure about that," she snaps.

I break an egg into the frying pan, wondering why I had washed it in the first place, put some bread in the toaster, and scrape the rest of the grits onto her plate, next to two links of sausage. She sits, rubbing her face.

Jesse points to his watch. "You know, we ate breakfast almost an hour ago."

"Well, good for you, Daddy."

That's how they've been since she got here, and it takes all the energy I can muster to steer them away from an out-and-out fight. It's hard work to make folks get along when they're dead set against it. I'd rather dig a ditch from here to Tallahassee. Jesse is kindhearted, deep down, but he can be a real instigator, too, like yesterday when he got into a tailspin because Rita didn't close the shower curtain. I thought he'd never stop harping on it—how it traps moisture and causes mildew. Now in all the years I've known him, I've never known him to give a fig about a shower curtain or mildew. He heard it on television is all, and wanted to use it to start an argument. He did that kind of thing to me, too, a long time ago, and it hurt my feelings, but then I wised up and let it run off me like water off a duck's back. But that's not Rita's nature.

I reach for her plate. "Here, let me heat that up for you," I say, but she holds it down with both hands.

"It's fine, Mama. Just sit down." Her eyelids are puffy and she looks tired.

"Did you sleep okay?" I ask. "That mattress ain't the best in the world." We bought it thirty-five years ago, when Jesse got his first paycheck working on a shrimp boat out of Port St. Joe.

She doesn't answer. She just stares at the jar of blackberry jelly like she's hypnotized and bites into a sausage link.

Jesse sits up, his chest curling over his stomach, and starts to cough. It's a terrible cough, and I hear it all day and night, even in my sleep. He knows it's bad but he still doesn't believe the emphysema will kill him, and maybe, Lord willing, it will be a while before it does. He scoots to the edge of the couch, wiping the water from his eyes, then gets up and walks to the refrigerator. More and more he reminds me of a turtle stripped of its shell, with his chin slipping into his neck and his skin paling to the color of a catfish's belly. He never was a big man, but he sure was handsome once, and as strong as men twice his size. It's such a peculiar thing to watch him failing so fast.

"That's a fine preacher," he says, removing the wrapper from a slice of cheese. He hardly touched his breakfast, so I'm surprised he wants it.

"Sounds like it," I tell him, but what I really want to say is that the preacher is giving me a headache right over my left eye and could you please turn it down.

He rolls up the cheese and takes a bite. "Did you tell Rita that her old man called?"

She looks at me. "He called while I was cooking breakfast," I say. I was going to tell her in private.

She tears off a piece of toast and drags it through the yolk. "What did *he* want?"

"He said he was bombing the fleas." She squints at me. "Well, what I mean is, he said to tell you he wouldn't be home because he was bombing the fleas."

"Did he say where Clint was?"

"No, and I didn't think to ask." Clint is her cat, the one she told us about on the way from the station, hinting to her daddy to take her to Tallahassee as soon as he would, to get him, but he told her no, he hates cats, which she already knew, and that a two-and-a half hour drive is longer than it used to be, especially with his back hurting.

"He said to tell you he'll be staying with a friend." She rolls her eyes and pushes her plate back. "You want some more milk?" I ask. "That two percent's pretty good once you get used to it, don't you think?"

Jesse frowns. "She can get her own milk. Her arms ain't broke."

I pour a glass, casting him a look, and he goes back to the couch.

"What makes him think I'm going over there anyway?" Rita says.

"I don't know, honey." The truth is, I don't know the man. He's from Virginia, and they've only been married a year, out of which he's been here once, at Christmas.

She blows her bangs from her eyes. The roots of her bleached hair have grown out, showing the real color, which is nearly as dark as her daddy's used to be, putting me in mind of a skunk. "Did he say anything else?"

"No."

I examine a tear I just found in the side seam of my shirt.

"I thought I'd make vegetable soup for supper," I tell her. She loves the okra, corn, and tomato soup I've made since she was little. "The only thing is I don't have fresh okra, so I'll have to use frozen, which isn't nearly as good."

A redbird flies so close to the window it startles me, then it curves around and lights in the cedar at the edge of the yard.

Rita is staring at the jelly again, rubbing her finger across the label. "Do you know if Jack Faison is still running the liquor store?" she asks.

I glance at Jesse to see if he heard. Even with the TV blaring, he's got good ears, but he's glued to every word the preacher is saying. The liquor store, which is also a bar, is a sore topic with him. He doesn't like it being down the road; he says it brings in the riffraff, and he was fit to be tied after Rita got a job there when she stayed with us before.

"I don't know," I say, running my fingernail down a groove in the table. Dirt flakes off, or maybe old polish. The wood is dark, so I couldn't have known it was there. Rita doesn't notice, but she's never been a housekeeper anyway, a trait she gets from her daddy's side. Me, I take after my mama and grandmama—I never could stand nastiness in any form. We may be poor, Mama always said, but as long as we have soap and water, we won't be dirty.

The kettle-shaped clock over the stove says nine-thirty by the time I finish the dishes. Rita has put on blue jeans that are laced up the sides with a black cord, showing her legs all the way up to her thighs, and a T-shirt with a pink teddy bear on it. Picking up her leather cigarette pouch, she walks past her daddy, who frowns at her pants, and heads out the back door. From the kitchen window, I watch her sit on the porch steps and pull out a cigarette, which she lights on the second try, wincing at the smoke as she gazes at the river.

I wish it was as simple to make her happy now as it was when she was growing up. We used to make lemon tea cakes like my granny made for me, and piece quilt tops together and do jigsaw puzzles. But ever since she left home, it seems like she's gone from one hard-luck situation to another, all her life. Bad luck with men mostly, they've always been her downfall, but even her son gives her nothing but trouble, stealing from her and running any old car she can get her hands on into the ground, and keeping her worried sick that he'll end up in the penitentiary—or worse.

I follow her outside, past Jesse who is watching another preacher now—a much younger one, with a wide face and short, curly blond hair—and I sit down beside her. "The sun feels good this morning," I say.

I used to sit out there a lot, listening to the birds singing and the leaves shimmying and watching the Spanish Moss floating on the breeze. I'd think about the river winding its way out to the bay and then all the way to the Gulf of Mexico. But these days, if I'm not cleaning or cooking, I sit with Jesse and pretend to be interested in his shows, because he doesn't like to be alone.

Up the river a piece, a motor cranks, and pretty soon an aluminum boat appears with two men that I don't recognize, but they wave and I wave back.

"Don't seem like a good day for fishing, does it? Too windy," I say.

Rita would know. She was quite the fisherman in her time. When she was only four or five, her daddy taught her to use a cane pole and to cast with a rod and reel when she wasn't much older. He showed her the best holes on the river—the big, deep ones—and he taught her how to gig frogs and set a trotline, too. And she could clean a fish faster than you could say Jack-spit-on-the-fire.

I couldn't count the times I'd watched them while I cooked, pulling the boat to the dock and climbing out laughing, having a big time. She always looked for me in the window and waved. Nobody looked happier than she did, running up the hill with a string of fish, her daddy strolling along behind her with the tackle box and poles.

We were proud of her, but we worried because she didn't like school. We figured it was a phase and that she'd pull up her grades before long, but she never did. "You're smarter than the whole lot of them," Jesse would tell her, but it didn't seem to sink in, and when she got pregnant, it like to have killed him. After that, they didn't fish anymore, and Jesse lost interest in the river.

Rita takes a pull off her cigarette and rests her forehead on her palm. "Just look at me, Mama. Old as I am and right back where I started."

"Oh, I wouldn't be too hard on myself, honey," I tell her, patting her leg. "Everybody has troubles now and then, but things have a way of working out, and they'll work out this time, too."

She grinds the cigarette out on the porch step with her flip flop. "You always say that. But somehow it never seems to happen."

***

A week later, I ride with Jesse to the specialist, because he hates going by himself, and I also need to get a few things. All the way home, he complains because the doctor didn't give him stronger pain pills. "He don't believe me when I tell him I'm hurting, but what does he know? He's too young to understand what pain is."

I don't doubt that Jesse has some, but if it was that bad, I would surely hear about it. He never could take pain. Once, when he stuck a fish hook in his hand, I had to dig it out, and even though it wasn't that deep, he passed out cold, which like to have scared me to death.

It's not just the doctor he's mad at. He's mad at Rita, too, because she never called her husband back. "He's going to wash his hands of her, just like I told you," he says. "And the next news you know, she'll be back working at that dive."

We turn off the river road and down the dirt lane to the house. As soon as I get out, I hear the pump running in the little house Jesse built around it. I wait for him to say it and sure enough he does: "Taking one of them two hour baths of hers again." Snatching his bag of aspirin and hemorrhoid ointment from the floorboard, he gets out and glares at me over the hood of the truck, telling me for the hundredth time that the pump is old and asking if I realize how much a new one costs these days. Then he stomps off to the house, leaving me to bring in the groceries.

I adjust the bags so that I have a free hand, and as soon as I open the door, cigarette smoke hits me in the face. Dread washes over me like cold molasses as I tote the bags to the table and put them down, wishing I was anywhere but here. The window over the sink is open even though the air conditioner is on, but the thick threads of smoke hang around the room without moving.

Jesse flies out of the bedroom, coughing, and scurries out the back door like the house is on fire. At the edge of the porch, he spits and coughs some more.

I hear the water shut off in the bathroom and the shower curtain slide open. "Oh Lord," I mutter, sawing open a bag of oranges with a steak knife and dumping them into a bowl, dropping one in the process. It rolls under the table, and I kneel to pick it up, just as Jesse storms back in, yanks the dish towel from the stove handle and starts flapping it around while he walks in circles, gasping like a fish out of water. Then he sets in to coughing again, throws the towel into the sink and stalks back to our bedroom.

There's a big commotion back there, as he pulls things from the closet, and pretty soon he comes back carrying the box fan that we use in the summer when we turn the air up at night. He shoves the plug into a socket and positions it on the floor in front of the stove, and when he turns it on high, the smoke begins to scatter.

"She didn't do it on purpose," I say. "She just wasn't thinking."

He grabs the remote, flops down on the couch and turns on the television.

Rita comes out shortly, her hair wet, wearing a denim skirt and a man's sleeveless undershirt with her bra showing through, a white one with tiny purple flowers. "What did the doctor say?" she asks, apparently not noticing the smoke, and there's enough electricity in the room to light up Atlanta.

Jesse springs off the couch with more energy than I've seen him have in years, and darts over to the kitchen table where she just sat down. "I'll tell you what he said!" he yells, his eyes bulging like a frog's. "He said don't you know you can't smoke in this house because your daddy's got emphysema? That's what he said!"

Her eyes get wide and she looks over at me. "Oh," she mumbles. "I'm sorry. I forgot, I guess."

He has another coughing fit, which makes him even madder, and he hits the table with the flat of his hand. "That's exactly right, Rita Jean, you just forgot, you just didn't think, and that's been your whole damn problem your whole damn life, from the time you laid down with that no-account Henderson boy until now, a blue million mistakes later."

She juts out her chin and glares at him for a few seconds, then looks out the window, pulling up the bra strap that has fallen down her arm. Her eyes well up and she starts to cry.

I wedge myself between them and put my arm around her. "That's enough, Jesse," I say, and I can tell by the look in his eyes that he knows he's gone too far.

She gets up and takes her cigarettes off the coffee table, then slams the back door behind her, while he goes out the front. Pretty soon I hear the truck crank and scratch out of the driveway, and I sigh and start putting up the rest of the groceries.

I catch a glimpse of Rita down by the river, just as she's turning onto a little trail that leads to an upstream sandbar, and I watch her disappear into the bushes. I wish she was climbing out of the boat with her Daddy, waving at me in the window. I wonder how things ever got in such a fix.

***

That night the three of us sit in the half-dark living room, watching a comedy show I can't make sense of, about people from another planet. Jesse's in his usual spot on the couch, and Rita's in the recliner next to my chair. She's sitting sideways, her face against the back of it, and she's not laughing, and neither is her daddy. All through supper, they didn't speak except for when he asked her to pass the salt.

His old cell phone rings so loud it nearly sends me through the roof, and I scramble up to answer it, because Jesse doesn't like to talk on the phone.

Any time there's a call after nine at night, I worry that it's bad news, that maybe my sister or some of her family is sick or dead. "Hello?" I say.

"Mrs. Rawlings?"

"Just a minute," I tell him. It's Rita's husband.

"I don't want to talk to him."

Her daddy rolls his eyes, and I just sit there holding the phone. "What do you want me to tell him then?"

"Tell him I'm not here," she says, loud enough for him to hear. I frown at her and shake my head, so she heaves a big sigh and takes it, then walks off down the hall.

"Well, at least they're talking," Jesse says.

About fifteen minutes later, she comes back, but I can't tell anything from her expression, and we all go back to watching TV. When the show finally goes off, Jesse asks, "How was Bill?"

"Fine," she answers and walks to the back door.

"Mosquitoes will eat you up out there," he tells her, poking the remote. He stops on a black-and-white show about a man rescuing a woman from some gangsters.

At ten o'clock, he turns it off, stands, and looks at me. "Well, I'm going on to bed. You coming?" He expects me to go when he does.

"No. I think I'll watch the rest of this movie," I say, reaching for the remote.

He shrugs. "Well, all right then."

Not long after he's gone to bed, Rita comes in and sits in the recliner, adjusting it until she's nearly stretched out straight. "Daddy still mad?"

"I don't think so."

She chews a thumb nail that's already down to the quick, like the rest of her fingernails. "I didn't smoke but one cigarette in here, I swear. I know he can't be around it, but I was on the phone with Jack about a job, and I guess... I guess I just didn't think... like he said."

"What about the job?" I ask, bracing for the answer.

"Oh, he doesn't need anybody right now, but he'll call if he does."

I'm relieved to hear it. I take off my nurse shoes, I call them, and put them on the floor beside the chair. They're the only kind that don't hurt my bunions, and I've nearly worn them out. "What did Bill say?"

She shrugs. "The same old stuff, you know."

"He misses you, I imagine."

"Yeah, I'd miss my slave, too, if I had one." The man on TV hugs the woman then kisses her. "Thanks for the cigarettes," Rita says. I sneaked them past Jesse while he was in the produce looking at collards. "I'll pay you back when I can. I asked Bill to send my income tax check when it comes, which should be soon. It was supposed to be here by now. I didn't work at that cafe all year for nothing."

She points at the trout on the wall next to the television. "Do you remember when Daddy caught that?" Before I can answer, she says, "It was right after my thirteenth birthday. I had started my period for the first time two days before that, so he wouldn't let me go."

I clearly remembered the day her period started. I hadn't thought of it in a long time, and when I did, I regretted that I'd handled it all wrong. I'd never really talked to her about women things, although I'd tried to once or twice. It was something my mama never talked to me about, so I didn't rightly know how.

They'd been out fishing, and I was defrosting the refrigerator, when she ran into the house with eyes as big as saucers. When I realized what had happened, I explained that it was something all girls went through every month. Then, I looked for a clean cotton rag for her to use until we could get to the store. She said that her stomach was pinching, so I gave her some aspirin and told her to lie down for a while. When Jesse came in, he asked if she was alright, but he wouldn't look at me. Female things had always embarrassed him.

She laughs a little and shakes her head. "That day in the boat, I said, 'Daddy, I think I've been cut or something!' Can you imagine being that dumb?" My eyes tear up, and she reaches over to touch my arm. "Aw, Mama, don't feel bad. Nobody ever told you either." I wipe my eyes, trying to smile. "But you know," she adds, "when Daddy realized what was wrong, he had the kindest look in his eyes. I knew his heart went out to me."

"He's always loved you, Rita. He just doesn't know how to show it sometimes, that's all."

"Yeah. I know, Mama," she says quietly.

***

The following week, a paper sack full of clothes and the old suitcase Jesse bought back when he worked offshore, sit on the floor by the couch, where he's lying as usual. He's watching two men hunt quail somewhere in Georgia with his mouth hanging open like a child watching cartoons. I can't help noticing that he's lost more weight, which isn't surprising, since he doesn't eat enough to keep a cricket alive. Sometimes he'll think of something for me to cook, something he's sure he could eat, but when I fix it, he doesn't want it after all.

Rita is in her bedroom, and I'm frying fish in my mama's big old cast iron skillet, the hushpuppies mixed and ready to drop in as soon as the fish are done. I slice a cucumber into a bowl, sprinkle on salt and pepper, pour vinegar over it and set it on the table. It's noon and although none of us ate much breakfast, I'm not hungry. I've lost some weight myself. The elastic in my pants is loose around my waist.

"Y'all come on and sit down now," I say, when the hushpuppies are done.

Jesse peels himself off the couch and shuffles to his chair at the end of the table, and before long, Rita comes in, sets a clear plastic bag full of makeup on top of the suitcase and joins us.

On the TV, they're talking about oversexed women who are married to men who don't like sex, and Jesse picks up the remote next to his plate and changes the channel. "You sure you don't want us to drive you?"

She takes a bite of fish and chews as she gazes out the window. "No. Thanks anyway. He's well on his way by now."

He nods, his chest whining like a north wind is whipping through it.

"It's a bluebird day, ain't it?" I say, filling her glass with tea.

Jesse stops eating and wipes his lips with a paper towel. "Little girl, I want you to know you can stay here as long as you need to. I hope you realize that."

I didn't expect that from Jesse, and I smile at him, sitting there so small in his chair.

"I appreciate it, Daddy," she says, putting her hand on his.

"But I do think you ought to give this thing a go," he adds, reaching for a hushpuppy. "Your fella seems okay to me, and you know there's two sides to every story."

When we're through, I stack the dishes while she runs water in the sink. "You go on and do what you need to," I say, gently pushing her out of the way. "I've got all day to do these dishes."

"Why don't y'all go fish a little when he gets here?" Jesse asks from the couch.

"He has to get back," Rita tells him. "He's helping somebody work on an engine."

I pile the dishes in the sink and follow her to the bedroom where I sit on the bed and watch her dry her hair. She's getting a little bit of a turkey neck, and her wrinkles are nearly as deep as mine, but in spite of that, she's still mighty pretty. She studies the part in her hair and frowns. "I need to stop at the drugstore and get some color."

When her hair is dry, she stuffs her cigarettes into a pocket of her shorts. "Want to walk down to the river?"

"Sure."

Outside the air smells like pine and the slightly swampy smell of the river, and the weather is as fair as a belle. We walk down to the water and sit on the grass by the dock, stretching our legs in front of us. On the far shore, a flock of blackbirds lights in a cypress, making a fuss. The sunshine is warm but not too hot, and I raise my face to it. It's good to be away from the television.

"Will you be alright?" I ask.

Leaning back on her hands, she looks at me, her pink lipstick spreading just a little into the tiny wrinkles around her lips. "Well, something has to work out sometime. It might as well be now." A white plane flies over, and I watch until it turns into a dot and disappears into the blue. Rita stands, wiping the back of her shorts. "Come on, Mama. Let's go for a ride."

"Lord, Rita, I wouldn't get in that old boat for love nor money. The motor probably won't crank anyhow. It hasn't been run in ages."

She climbs in the boat and checks the gas in the motor, then she yanks the cord. To my surprise, it sputters to a start. "It's fine, see? And besides, we have the paddles." She shuts it off, gets out and starts up the slope. "I'll tell Daddy we're going. Are the life jackets still in the shed?"

When she gets back, she holds the boat still while I step in, waiting until I'm seated. Then she jumps in and pulls on the old motor cord again. Smoke clouds around it, thick with the smell of gas, but it doesn't start this time. All the same, she keeps trying. I feel a little relieved that it won't crank, but just as I'm about to stand up and get out, it starts again—feebly at first, but then it strikes a steady hum.

She pushes us from the dock and points us upstream. The wind is a little chilly but not too bad with the sun on us. Waves fan out from the boat to the shore lined with cypresses, oaks and pines, and above us, a hawk circles, not bothering to beat its wings.

By the time we round the first bend, it dawns on me how much I've missed being on the river. Lord only knows the times me and Jesse went up and down it over the years, fishing and talking, eating sardines and crackers, and laughing. He always could say the funniest things and kept me in stitches nearly all the time. Even when I was pregnant, it didn't hinder us any. We felt so good in our bodies back then, our skin tan and our eyes bright and clear. We had our whole lives ahead of us, and getting old or sick never entered our minds.

Rita's hair blows around her face, and there's a calm look in her eyes. Now and then she looks at me and smiles, but we don't try to talk over the noise of the motor. We ride along, content to be quiet. Occasionally, I point to a heron on a dead cypress or a little alligator sunning on the bank. Farther on, a few more bends up the river, a sturgeon leaps into the air and falls back in with a big splash. Rita slows the boat. She knows that you have to be careful of those things. One slammed into Jesse's uncle years ago and broke his arm. Jesse said he'd been driving his boat too fast, though, and standing up besides.

In ten or fifteen minutes, we reach a sign that says "Smokehouse Landing," and Rita makes a wide turn to head back downstream. It takes us into our own wake, which makes the boat skip over the waves, bouncing us and making us laugh. Then she reaches back and switches off the motor.

I close my eyes for a little bit and listen to the water lapping at the boat and the pine tops swishing in the breeze.

"Daddy's a lot worse, ain't he?" she says.

"Yes, I reckon he is," I answer, opening my eyes. A turtle drops off a log as we get close, sloshing the water a little.

"I know it's hard on y'all. It breaks my heart to lose him."

I nod and untie my shoes, slipping them off and letting the sun warm my feet.

"I'll come help when it's time."

"That'll be good."

She watches the hawk that's still overhead and maneuvers the paddles from time to time. I reach over the side of the boat to feel the water. It's cool but not too cold.

"You know, Mama," she says, finally, "I realize I'm the biggest part of the problem—in my relationships, that is."

"Well, like your daddy says, there's always two sides to every story."

"Yeah, I know. But it's mostly me." She sighs loudly. "And I'm just so tired of the drama, you know? I'm too old for it anymore."

"But you said he didn't treat you too good."

She frowns. “I don’t know why I said that, because it’s not true. I guess I was just making excuses.”

“Well, do you love him?”

She laughs a little. “I think I really do. And I believe I’m finally starting to understand about commitment. You know, real commitment...like you and Daddy. I can’t just give up and run off every time the wind blows.”

I nod. “That’s true, Rita. You know, marriage ain’t no cakewalk sometimes, but you’ve got to stand by one another.”

She smiles a big smile at me and I smile back. “I’m going to work on it this time, Mama. I mean it.”

“Well, it sure makes me happy to hear that, honey,” I say. And we drift on home, just taking in the scenery.

BETTER BY NOW

Down by the water, a little girl in a blue bathing suit shovels sand into a pail, paying no attention to the children around her, or to the plane flying overhead towing a yellow banner. Now and then, a strip of hair blows across her eyes, and she stops to brush it away, but even then she doesn't look up until the bucket is full. When it is, she turns it upside down and carefully lifts it from a cone of sand. "Look, Mommy!" she says.

A young woman under a yellow-striped umbrella lowers her book and smiles. "Oh that's wonderful, honey! It's the most beautiful sandcastle I've ever seen!"

Next to me, my best friend, Julie, sighs and nudges me with her shoulder. "You haven't heard a thing I've said, Ellie. I know I'm not the most entertaining person in the world, but you could at least act like you're listening." She props her head on her hand and stares at me.

"I heard you," I told her. "You were talking about Hunter's new girlfriend." Hunter is her ex-husband, a womanizing asshole.

She follows my gaze to the little girl, and I know what she's thinking. She's thinking that I'm obsessing about Chloe again. "Would you hand me the suntan lotion?" I ask.

The fake coconut smell of it is a little nauseating, but I don't want to burn, so I slather it all over, lie back, and close my eyes, listening to the sea gulls and people and music and the cars driving by on the four-lane just over the dunes. A bead of sweat slides down my temple into my hair, and I drape a towel over my face. It feels good to get out of the sun.

Julie turns onto her stomach, humming along with a song that's playing a few yards away. "Hey, El?"

"Yeah?" I answer through the towel.

"You want to go somewhere tonight? Maybe get a pizza?"

I don't want to do anything but watch TV and go to bed early. I didn't want to come here in the first place. But as soon as I stepped off the plane in Pensacola, my mom started in. "You know my friend, Linda, from the church choir? Well, she has that lovely condo in Destin, and she has offered to let you use it. I thought you and Julie might like to spend a few days at the beach." I can easily imagine what she said to Julie, too: "Maybe you can talk to her, honey. I know a year isn't all that long, especially when something this tragic happens, but don't you think she should be better by now?"

Ben was certainly happy to hear we were going. "The salt air and sunshine will do you good, babe," he said, like California didn't have those. He's frustrated and doesn't know what to do anymore. He took me to Big Bear, skiing, he bought me jewelry, he even threw a surprise birthday party for me, but nothing made me feel better for long. I just couldn't come to terms with what happened, not even slightly, and I was angry at him for taking our baby's death like a marine—the way he made the funeral arrangements, the way he interacted with our friends, the way he put on his flight suit and went to work each day—with a stiff upper lip and a pull-yourself-up-by-the-bootstraps attitude.

The last year had been hazy and confusing, completely opposite my usual structured life. When he was home, I made an effort to cook and keep the house presentable, and he helped with that, but when he was deployed or at the base, I mostly stayed in bed. Week after week and month after month, I stared into space, trying to figure out what I had done wrong. All during my pregnancy, I'd read every baby book I could find, and gleaned advice from friends with children, determined to be the best mother I could be. When we brought Chloe home, I made sure she slept on her back and that there was never anything in the crib that could choke her. I breast fed her and kept the temperature just right while she slept. How could a healthy baby just stop breathing like that? *What* could cause such a thing?

Three weeks after she died, Ben took the crib away, to put it in storage, and I couldn't stop crying. "Ellie," he said, holding me by the shoulders and looking into my eyes, "it's not good for you to see it every day. I'm only trying to help. Please let me help you." A few times, we had gone to the Sudden Infant Death Syndrome support group, because he wanted to, but it only made me feel worse to listen to the stories and watch people cry. Knowing that others shared my grief should have made me feel better, I supposed, but it didn't.

"Well, do you?" Julie asks. "Do you want to go do something tonight?"

I push the towel away and squint at the hotels down the shoreline. Someone is parasailing over the water in front of them, their legs dangling. "Yeah, I guess we could."

I know she must be sick of hanging around the condo watching TV all day and night, or sitting out on the balcony watching people on the beach, much of the time while I'm sleeping. It's a treat for her to be here. It's not easy for the cancer ward to do without her, and her mother has taken time off from work to keep the kids. Julie's job isn't easy and neither is raising two kids practically by herself.

Out of nowhere, a frisbee comes whirling toward us ninety to nothing, and just as I open my mouth to tell Julie to watch out, it hits her shoulder.

A guy in red shorts runs up with a concerned look on his face. He looks like a surfer, tan and sinewy, with wavy blond hair nearly to his shoulders. "Oh man!" he says, "I am *so* sorry! Are you all right?"

She hands him the frisbee and smiles. "I'm fine. No problem."

"Are you sure?"

"I'm sure."

He puts his hand to his chest. "I'm really glad. It's hard to play when it gets this crowded. I think we better move up closer to the dunes." He starts to leave but turns back around. "Hey, do you guys want to play?"

"No thanks," I say, but Julie doesn't hesitate. She was probably hoping he would ask.

She jumps up, adjusting her polka-dot bikini bottom, and looks down at me. "Come on, El! It'll be fun! How long has it been since you threw a frisbee?"

"Not long enough. But you go ahead." She follows him and they join two of his friends who are standing in front of a pop-up tent.

I marvel at how easily she throws, her blond ponytail swinging, and I can tell by the way the guys look at each other, they're just as impressed. She has always been athletic. In high school, she was on the volleyball team and the swim team, too, and she's still in terrific shape. She could almost pass for their age—probably early 20s—though she's a decade past that.

Forty-five minutes later, I'm half asleep when she returns, out of breath and laughing. "Ellie, this is Ray-Ray," she says, nodding to the guy who asked us to play. "Ray-Ray, this is Ellie. We've been best friends since first grade."

Why does he need to know that, I wonder, and what kind of name is Ray-Ray?

He stretches out his hand. "Nice to meet you. Julie tells me you're from California."

"Nice to meet you, too. No, I just live there."

"She says you're married to a marine pilot. That's cool. My stepbrother is in the air force." He looks down the beach toward the jetty, and rakes his hair back with both hands. "Well, I guess I'll get going. I hope to see you guys tonight." Then he runs to catch up with his friends who are walking toward the hotels.

"Isn't he yummy?" she says. "Oh my God! If I were that age again, he would be my type." She smiles and winks at me. "But then I'm not looking to get married, right?"

"Go where tonight?"

"Oh, some place across the bridge." She rubs lotion on her face and puts the bottle back in the bag, then she tightens her ponytail.

"What kind of place?"

"Well, actually, it's a bar... but we could still get pizza first." She's waiting for me to respond, but I don't. "Well?" she says, finally.

"Well what?"

"Well, do you want to?

"That would be a no," I say. The last thing I want to do is stand around a bar with a bunch of kids, watching them get wasted.

She makes a sound between a grunt and a sigh. "Oh, come on, it's Friday! What else are we going to do, watch another stupid movie?"

"You can go without me. Seriously, it won't hurt my feelings one bit."

She puts on her sunglasses, rifles through the beach bag and takes out her phone. "Nah. That's all right. I really don't care that much about it anyway." She finds an old Maroon 5 song, holds the phone to her ear, and gazes out at the gulf.

I watch her for a couple of minutes, then sigh and pull myself up. "Okay then, if you want to go that badly, we'll go."

She grins and tosses the phone on the blanket. "Awesome! It'll be fun, you'll see, and if it's not, we'll just leave."

Before long, we decide that we're close to burning, so we scoop up the sheet and the beach bag and head to her car. On top of a dune, I stop and, shielding my eyes, I turn and search for the little girl with the bucket, but she's nowhere to be seen. And all traces of her sandcastle have been erased by the tide.

***

The music is so loud the walls are vibrating. "I don't see them," Julie yells into my ear.

"It's only nine-thirty. That's early to them, I imagine."

She lifts my arm and looks at my watch, as if I hadn't just told her the time. "Come on," she says, grabbing my elbow, and pulls me to the bar. "I know what we need."

I stare at a neon palm tree while she orders, wondering what I'm doing here. By now, Ben has finished his five-mile run, taken a shower, and is watching the news. I left him a message before we went to the pizza place, letting him know that we were going out. What would he think if he saw me here, surrounded by wannabe surfers and skinny girls with rings in their noses? He'd be glad I was doing something besides sleeping, I was sure.

Julie points across the room. "There's an empty table."

It's close to the dance floor, which is a big, raised platform with brass bars around it, on which a few people are dancing, though what they're doing looks a lot more provocative than dancing. Now and then, steam shoots up through the floor, giving the whole scene the appearance of Hell. I take a long drink of margarita and pull out a chair.

"Look!" Julie says, "There's Ray-Ray!"

Sure enough, he's standing in the entrance, dressed in ripped, faded jeans and a Billabong T-shirt. He walks to the bar, speaking to a couple of people on the way, then he orders a drink, leans against the bar, and scans the room. When he sees us, he grins, raises his beer, and saunters over.

"Where are your friends?" she asks.

"Oh, they went bungee jumping." He laughs. "Well, one actually jumps, the other is afraid of heights, but they'll be by later, I'm sure." He nods at an empty chair across from us. "May I?"

They chat while I sip my drink and watch the lights flash around the periphery of the dance floor. Excusing myself, I head to the restroom, where I stand in line with 20-somethings who are discussing hair, makeup, and men. They are pretty in their short dresses and heels and their flawless foundation over their flawless skin, and I wonder if they realize how beautiful they are. Probably not, if they're as self-conscious as I was at that age.

My phone vibrates, and I take it from my pocket. It's Ben, so I leave the line and stand in the corner to talk to him. He asks how I'm doing, and I say fine and I ask how he's doing. Our phone conversations are stilted, no different from when we're together, but when he asks where I am, and I tell him, he laughs. "That's great, honey," he says, genuine relief in his voice. He tells me that his squadron is leaving for Fallon, Nevada in the morning, and he'll call me the next night. "Hey, don't let those young dudes get too friendly now," he says, then he admonishes me not to drive, like I would, and I tell him we're taking an Uber. Before he hangs up, he says "I love you, Ellie Grace."

"Okay then," I say. "You have a safe trip." After a pause, he hangs up.

Julie and Ray-Ray are dancing when I get back, or rather they're talking as they walk in little circles. After the dance, she tells me she'll be right back, and before long, she returns with a shot of something red and plops it down in front of me. My first impulse is to decline, but then I think what the heck, I haven't been out in a long time, and it might just make this night bearable. The cinnamon flavor tastes good, but it burns my nose.

"Why don't you two dance?" Julie asks, and Ray-Ray gives me a questioning look.

I shake my head. "Oh, no thanks. I really don't want to."

He stands, laughing, and takes my hand. "That's not the right answer."

I feel even more out of place on the dance floor. I don't dance like the others, I'm not dressed like them, in my jeans and sandals and white T-shirt, and I'm older than they are, too, although looking around, I notice a few people my age as well. These young girls think I'm a cougar, no doubt, not realizing that I'm about as close to that as I am to being the cat. I close my eyes and try to get into the beat, but it's sort of rappy and hard to dance to, and when it's over, I'm relieved, and I hurry back to the table before another song starts.

I spot Julie at the bar, talking to a guy in a baseball cap, and I wonder what Ray-Ray thinks about it, but he doesn't seem to notice. The waitress asks if we want another round, and I order another margarita, promising myself that I will nurse it, because I'm beginning to feel the first one, along with the shot.

Before long, Julie comes back with another one, this time tequila with lemon and salt. I refuse to drink it, so she shrugs and downs it herself. Once more, she says she'll be back soon, but the way she wiggles her eyebrows at me tells me I shouldn't hold my breath. I motion her over. "What about him?" I say into her ear, hoping Ray-Ray can't hear.

"The guy at the bar is my age, and more my type," she says into mine. I don't think Julie knows what her type is. "Besides, he's not interested in me anyway. Not like that."

I drink my margarita, nodding to the music, which is sounding better, while Ray-Ray smiles and taps his fingers on the table. I don't believe he has stopped smiling since I met him, and I wonder if he's on something. "You sure do smile a lot," I say over the table.

He stops tapping and leans in. "What's that?"

"I said, don't you ever stop smiling?"

He throws his head back and laughs. "I don't know. I've never thought about it. I guess I do sometimes."

The DJ is encouraging everyone to get on the dance floor, which is already packed, but we decide to join them. As soon as we step onto the platform, a girl with long dark hair and a ring in her eyebrow sidles up to Ray-Ray and gives him a long, seductive look. He doesn't respond, and it suddenly occurs to me that he thinks we are going to do more than dance. Why else would he spend the evening with us—with me? Maybe he's into older women and married ones at that.

As soon as we sit, I motion him over. "I'm afraid you're wasting your night on me," I tell him, hoping he gets my point.

He looks at me funny. "How do you mean?"

I sip my drink, peering at him over the salted rim. "I think you know what I mean."

He grins, revealing a dimple I hadn't noticed on the left side of his chin. "Oh, I get it. You're referring to my uncontrollable animal urges."

Before I can answer, the other two frisbee players appear at the entrance, and Ray-Ray waves at them. They stop at the bar before coming to the table to sit, and Ray-Ray introduces us. They tell us about the bungee jump and some guy they know who backed out at the last moment. The jumper, who is Australian, tells me it's a real rush, and I should try it sometime, then he holds up his beer and toasts his country. Though I've never been, I join in, glancing at my watch.

By now Ben is lying on the couch watching a rerun of M*A*S*H* or maybe the news again. I wonder if he misses me. Probably no more than when I'm there with him... maybe even less. I lick salt from my glass and take a long drink.

Julie partly walks and partly dances back to the table with the guy from the bar and introduces him to everyone. He is athletic, too, likely a bodybuilder from the look of his chest and arms. I tell him it's nice to meet him, then I wind my way through the crowd and back to the ladies room, where, after waiting in line again, I close the stall door behind me. Some girls at the sink are talking about a guy named Howl, or at least that's what I think they're calling him.

"Are you okay in there?" asks Julie, her feet appearing under the door.

The tissue tears off in little strips. "Yes, I'm fine."

She taps on the door. "Are you sure?"

"Sure I'm sure. What makes you think I'm not?"

I feel tipsy but it's nice. I fumble with the lock and finally open the stall door, and the girls stare at us like we're monkeys in a zoo as they make room for me at the sink. I glance at Julie, and we start to giggle, and in no time we're laughing so hard we're having to hold each other up. Before we leave, I tell them to say hi to Howl for me, and even though Julie has no idea what I'm talking about, she falls into hysterics anyway

***

Ray-Ray and I are sitting on his T-shirt, watching the moon ride the waves, taking a drink of hot beer every now and then. Julie and the bar guy went to get it, and now they're making out on the other side of a dune behind us. I'm grateful that the waves are drowning out most of the noise.

Ray-Ray tells me that his mother lives in West Palm Beach, and that she's hooked up with a loser. He says she always hooks up with losers, but he loves her a lot and worries about her all the time. He says her last husband threw hot grease on her years ago, when Ray-Ray was eleven, which scarred her neck and chest. She's had plastic surgery for it, but you can still see the scars. His father owns three restaurants and lives in a big house not too far away, and plays golf and drinks vodka most of the time. Ray-Ray lives with him and works at one of the restaurants while he goes to college. He got a late start, but now he knows it was a good idea. He says his father wants him to run the business one day, but he wants to be a marine biologist... and surf.

"Someplace where they have real waves, like Australia, or maybe Hawaii."

"I can see you doing that," I tell him.

Way out over the water, a plane flies by, and I watch until its lights fade.

"Julie told me about your little girl," he says softly. "I'm really sorry."

Before I can stop myself, tears flood my eyes and I let out a sob. I'm appalled by my sudden outburst, and I hold my hand over my mouth.

"Oh, man, I'm so sorry!" he says. "It was stupid of me to bring it up."

I clear my throat and try to reign in my emotions, embarrassed to behave this way in front of someone I hardly know. Why did Julie even mention it to him? She had no right. But I know she meant no harm. "It's all right."

"No. No, it's not. Please forgive me. It's none of my business."

Down the beach, in the hotel light, two people walk into the water and fade into the dark waves. In the far distance, a tower blinks red.

"We had her for such a short time," I say quietly.

Ray-Ray leans closer and nods.

Tears begin to stream down my face, and words spill out, too. I tell him everything. I tell him that I miss her more than anyone will ever know and that I still talk to her and take out her clothes and smell them. I tell him that I found her lifeless body in her crib by our bed when I woke up that morning, and the shock of it shattered me into a million pieces. The grief is so overwhelming, I feel like I'm drowning, and I can't find my way back to safety, to peace, to life, no matter how I try. I tell him I'm afraid I'll never learn to live without her, that it seems impossible, and I'm angry because my husband has gone on as if nothing ever happened.

When I'm finished, he puts his hand on mine, and we sit in silence for a while, listening to the waves caressing the shore.

"Maybe," he says finally, "he's just as hurt as you are, but he's trying to be strong for you. You know, like a lighthouse in a storm."

I wipe my face with the bottom of my shirt and smile a little. "You know, you're pretty wise for your years, Ray-Ray."

Stretched out before us, as far as our eyes can see, the water is glorious, with the angel-white moon casting its light on the waves like a net of diamonds. I breathe in the salt air, relishing the enduring breeze. The gulf is so familiar, so healing, and its music is a lullaby I've loved since I was a little girl. But it's time now, I know, to go back to California.

SOMEBODY NEEDING WATER

I'm dreaming that a woman in a mink coat is shoving me into a tiny closet, when the smoke alarm goes off. Carl and I sit straight up in bed and look at each other, then at the same time, we throw back the covers and fly down the hall to the other end of the trailer, where smoke is coming out of Daddy's room. He is standing just inside the door, poking at the detector with a broom handle, but I don't take the time to tell him to cut that out. I just shove past him to the bed.

It's on fire. It's not a raging fire, just a few low flames on the old mattress, and a good chunk of the plastic wicker headboard has melted, but it's plenty bad enough. Carl grabs a blanket and slaps it against the mattress, and, holding the sleeve of my gown to my nose, I snatch back the curtains and open the window. In just a few licks, the fire is out, and I lean against the door, holding my hand to my chest, telling myself to calm down now, it's over. "Fifty-year-old women frequently die of heart attacks, Mrs. Baines," my doctor told me, and he said I should really think about that. He said I should eat right and lose weight, too, but that's easy for him to say. He doesn't have a daddy who's dying of cancer living with him and a husband who's mad about him being there.

I take a few long breaths and tell myself that everything is fine, but my heart isn't having it. It's jarring against my rib cage so hard it feels like it's going to bust out of there, and my hands are shaking like a leaf in a windstorm.

Carl is staring down at the bed, smut streaked across his chin, holding the charred blanket and panting like a hunting dog. "What the hell were you thinking, Lonnie?" he yells, but Daddy is nowhere to be seen. He throws the blanket on the floor as hard as he can and bends down to pick up something he sees on the other side of the bed. "Well, I guess we know how it started," he says, holding up a pack of cigarettes and shaking it at me.

"Just calm down, honey," I say, rubbing his chest, but he's not having it. Leaning out the door, I look down the hallway. "Daddy, get in here!" I holler, and pretty soon he appears, his old slippers flapping as he shuffles toward me.

"Yeah?" he says, all mild-mannered, like he can't imagine why I called him in there, but his eyes are uneasy.

"Daddy," I say, "do you realize how dangerous it is to be smoking in here? Sick or not, you can't go around nearly burning people up in their beds. Do you understand that you could have burned us alive? And what in the world were you doing smoking cigarettes anyway?"

He blinks and looks at his feet. Carl is chewing his bottom lip, glaring at him. Daddy starts to cough and pretty soon it's a regular fit. I wet a towel in the bathroom, ring it out, and swoosh it around the room, trying to clear the smoke, then I turn on the box fan in the corner. When his coughing finally stops, he nods at me and says he knows it's dangerous and he's sorry.

"Well, sorry ain't good enough," says Carl, and for a second, anger flickers in Daddy's eyes, but just as quickly, it's gone. Carl looks at me. "He's your daddy. You straighten it out."

In the harshest tone I can muster, I say, "Carl is right, you know. There's no excuse for this. You know good and well that we can't afford to buy new beds or new trailers. Hell, we don't even have insurance on this one. Where would we all be if this place had gone to ashes?"

He rubs his eyes, looking so dried-up in his thin, white T-shirt and pajama pants with "#1 Dad" written all over them, and I just can't be mean. Besides, I'm too damn tired.

I put my hands on his shoulders, and look into his eyes. "I know you didn't mean it, Daddy, but please please don't pull a stunt like this again."

"I won't. I promise. And I'll pay for the bed, too."

Carl's face is as red as a rooster's comb, the birthmark over his right eye dark purple, and for a minute I wonder what I ever saw in him, he's so ugly. But it's only when he's mad. Except for his big belly, Carl's a tall, fine-looking man who I'm proud to call my husband. I've only seen him this mad once before, and that was when his daughter called and said her boyfriend had hit her. In the middle of the night, he had packed a change of clothes in a paper sack and drove straight over to Atlanta, and although I never knew exactly what happened, I know she never complained about her boyfriend again.

It's not Carl's fault. He has every right to be pissed. Daddy could be such a pill, and setting a bed on fire is no laughing matter. I'm pretty sure Carl knows Daddy doesn't like him much anyway. Daddy made that plain, at least to me, three years ago when I told him I was getting married.

It was Easter, and we were on our way to put flowers on Mama's grave, some yellow lilies we picked up at the dollar store, and he didn't utter a word until we got to the cemetery, then he opened the car door, looked back at me and shook his head. "Lorraine," he said with a loud sigh, "you're making a mistake getting mixed up with this Baines fellow. From the first time I clapped eyes on him, I knew he was just a big bag of hot air."

I wanted to say "I don't know if you've noticed, Daddy, but I ain't exactly in no prime position to land a doctor or a lawyer. In the first place, there aren't any decent men around anymore, and all the ones my age are out chasing girls thirty years younger." He didn't know what it was like to be divorced for eleven years, and spend weekend after weekend at home with him, watching reruns of Sanford and Son or The Beverly Hillbillies. He didn't know how it felt to sit in a bar, on the rare occasions I went out with a friend, scanning faces for someone who could see past my teased hair, snug jeans, and sparkly shirt, to my heart. No, he wanted to keep me with him, cooking and cleaning and driving him to appointments, and that's all that seemed to matter.

"Carl's a good man, Daddy," I told him. "You just need to give him a chance." And I meant every word of it. He was a good man. Is a good man. "He's done a lot for me, and for you, too," I said. "Who put down that new pump? Who keeps the yard mowed and the garden plowed? Doesn't that count for anything?"

Apparently it didn't, but I don't hold things like that against him, it's just his nature, like it's mine not to hold grudges. That's not to say that I forget things. It's just that I don't like harboring ill will toward anybody. Over the years, I've said hateful things to people, and they've said hateful things to me, but I like to think we forgave each other and moved on.

"Let's get out of this smoke," I say, and we head to the living room, Carl stomping behind us. Daddy's breathing sounds like somebody sucking the last drops of Coke from a can with a straw. Taking his arm, I lead him to the couch and begin making little karate chops on his back, like the therapist showed me. The first time I did it, I could tell by the look on her face that I wasn't doing it right, but I was afraid to hurt him. He's so frail, with his bony back and his jaybird chest all caved in.

"You have to do it harder. You've got to loosen the phlegm so they can cough it up," she said, talking like he wasn't in the room.

That was the day after I brought him home from the hospital. The doctor said Daddy couldn't stay by himself any longer, that me or my sister would have to take care of him, or he'd send him to a nursing home. "You understand," the doctor said out in the hallway, "that I'm sending him home to die."

It put me in a real quandary when he told me that, though I knew it was coming. On one hand, there was Carl, and things were going so good for us. We were finally putting back a little money, what with my job at the laundromat and his raise at the trucking company, although Daddy being there wouldn't change that part since he had his own check. But we were just happy by ourselves. We fished and camped, and we liked to lounge around the house half-dressed. Now I would be taking care of Daddy again. Full time.

Still, I couldn't let him die in a nursing home. It would have been different if his mind was bad, and he didn't know where he was anyhow. I had been lucky with Mama in that department, since she died in the hospital right after her stroke. Of course my sister wouldn't help with Daddy. She lived in Tennessee, and she hadn't even been to see him the whole time he was in the hospital. She said it was too far to drive, and what could she do anyway, she wanted to know. So standing there with the doctor that afternoon, I told him I'd bring Daddy home with me when he released him the next day. Carl would just have to deal with it. After all, it was only for a little while. How bad could it be?

I'm glad I didn't know how bad it could be, because if I had, I would've run through the hospital parking lot, screaming and pulling my hair out. That night, we had the worst fight of our marriage, both of us saying some awful things, and in the end, he said I should send Daddy to my sister whether she liked it or not. He said I'd already done my part and then some, taking care of him for so long after Mama died.

"But, Carl, Daddy don't want to die in Tennessee. He wants to die in Alabama, where he was born and raised. You can understand that. I know you can."

He looked me in the eyes and said, "Well, I don't see why he can't go up there until he's almost dead and then come back down here."

I pound Daddy's back with the flat of my hand, but not too hard. "You know you shouldn't be smoking," I say, "and you with lung cancer, for heaven's sake." Daddy doesn't realize the cancer's all over his body. The doctor told him, but he was so hopped up on whatever they had in his IV, it didn't register, which is probably for the best. I reach over and tear some paper towels from a roll on the end table and hold them to his mouth so he can spit up the yellow-brown mucus. His eyes are watering so much it looks like he's crying.

It's nearly midnight, so I get some sheets and blankets to make up the couch, and bring in his fan, which I put on the floor in front of him. "We'll sleep with the air off tonight," I say, opening more windows and cranking up the ceiling fans. "None of us need to be cooped up in this smoke."

Carl is leaning against the sink in his boxers, drinking a beer, watching me pull the covers to Daddy's neck. He shoots me an irritated look, takes another beer from the refrigerator, and heads out the back door, letting it bang behind him.

I open it and look out. "Ain't you coming to bed, hon? You need to get some sleep. You've got your Georgia run in the morning."

"Ain't sleepy." The moon is almost full, but I can't see him.

I switch off the lamp beside the couch, and gently push what's left of Daddy's hair from his damp forehead. "Don't worry about nothing," I whisper. "Everything will be all right."

In our bedroom, I change into one of Carl's big white T-shirts and peek out the window. He's on the porch now, in a lawn chair with his feet propped on the railing. For a minute I think of going out there, but I've been up since 5:00 that morning, and I have to open the laundromat at 6:00. He rests his head against the back of the chair and recrosses his feet. He appears to be staring at the moon.

***

When I get home from work a few days later, I'm glad to see Carl's semi parked on the stretch of clay out by the pump house, even though I'm ticked that he didn't call me even once while he was gone. Things are a little tense between us right now, but it's nothing that can't be remedied. I park the car and listen to Waylon sing "I Ain't Living Long Like This" before I roll up the windows and get out. I've decided to take the high road. I'll go in there and fry up some pork chops, Carl's favorite, and make him some rice and gravy and biscuits, then after Daddy goes to sleep, I'll put on my red shorty nightgown and make him forget we had ever been fighting.

He's in his recliner when I walk in, watching the news with a remote in one hand and a beer propped on his stomach in the other, and Daddy is asleep on the couch. Daddy's cheeks are so red they look painted on, even though the AC is running, and the ceiling fan is full tilt above him. Setting my purse on the kitchen table, I switch on the box fan and turn it toward him, then I lean over and kiss the top of Carl's head. "Hey baby," I say.

"The AC is on," he says.

"What?"

"I said the air conditioner is on," he repeats, like he's talking to someone who can't speak English.

"I know it is. What do you mean?"

"Well, you don't need all these fans going with the AC on," he tells me, not looking away from the TV. "The electric bill is high enough as it is."

"Daddy's burning up, Carl!" I snap.

He mutes the TV and looks at me. "I'm sorry, Lorrie. I'm just tired, I reckon." He slaps his knee for me to come sit. "Hey, are you off tomorrow?"

"I sure am."

"Want to go fishing then?

"Oh baby, I can't. I've got a hair appointment at 10:30." He looks at the ceiling and sighs like it's the end of the world. "I'd cancel it, but it needs cutting so bad." I point to my scalp. "Just look at these roots."

"That's okay. Just forget it."

"Maybe we can go next weekend? I'll see if Roxanne can come." Roxanne is one of the hospice volunteers who comes when I have to work and Carl can't be home. I reach up and wrap my arms around his neck, planting a kiss on him that gets his attention, and he begins to perk up real fast.

"Let's go to the back," he whispers, kissing my neck.

"We can't right now, honey," I say, pulling his hand from my bra. "Just wait until a little later, all right? After Daddy's gone to bed."

He stops cold and pushes me off his lap with more force than he ought to, then he jumps up and strides to the kitchen. With one swipe of his arm, he clears the counter, sending my red-flowered canisters, a coin-filled Mason jar, and a little bowl of butterscotch candy flying everywhere. After that, he storms out the front door, leaving me standing there with my mouth wide open, flour falling around me like snow, not believing what I just saw.

Daddy is sitting up, wild-eyed. "What's wrong? What happened?"

"Nothing," I tell him, trying to sound normal. "I just dropped some things, that's all. You go on back to sleep."

He glances at the mess on the floor and looks at me funny, but puts his head back on the pillow. I sigh, get the broom and begin to clean up, wiping tears and listening to the blood rush through my head like Niagara Falls. Outside, the car cranks, and I watch it tear off in a dust cloud.

***

Carl didn't come home all night, and I'm on the front porch steps the next morning drinking coffee with hands so jittery I can barely hold the cup. I've spilled it all over the front of my gown, and I don't care enough to wash it out before it stains. Daddy just finished his breakfast, what little of his oatmeal he ate, and he's already asleep on the couch.

I don't know what to do. Half of me is so mad I could spit nails, and the other half is worried that Carl is wrapped around a pine somewhere.

At 8:00, I call his mother, but before I can even say good morning, she is rattling on about the neighbor's dog digging up her roses, saying she's going to shoot him if he does it again, and the neighbors, too, if they're not careful.

"Is Carl over there?" I ask, finally getting a word in edgewise.

She gets quiet then, greedy for gossip, no matter if it involves her own son. "No... is he supposed to be?"

I tell her I must have misunderstood where he said he was off to this morning. There's another long pause as she tries to decide if I'm telling the truth.

"No, I haven't seen him, but he needs to get his butt out here and fix my pump house like he promised he would a month ago."

When I hang up, I try his brother, but he doesn't answer and his voicemail is full, so I stare into the cloudless sky, wondering where in the blazes Carl could be, getting madder by the minute. My stomach feels like it's been sucker punched.

Thirty minutes later, I'm looking out the kitchen window as I wash up the breakfast dishes, and the car pulls up. Carl gets out and glances at me, but when he comes in he doesn't say a word and heads straight to the bedroom. As soon as I can squeeze out the dish sponge and dry my hands, I follow him.

He's lying with his arm over his face, still dressed in the clothes he had on yesterday, and smelling like a distillery. He hasn't even taken off his boots.

"Where have you been?" I ask.

"Nowhere."

"Well, you sure as hell haven't been here, I can tell you that. Where did you stay last night, Carl?"

He turns on his side away from me and pulls a pillow over his head. "Mama's," he mumbles, or at least that's what I think he said.

"I talked to her this morning, so don't lie to me."

He throws the pillow aside, sits up, and pulls off a boot, still not making eye contact. "Don't start with me, Lorraine," he snarls, tossing the boot through the open closet door. "If you just got to know, I was at The Night Owl until it closed, and then I fell asleep in the car at Wayside Park." He takes off the other boot and lies back down, facing the wall again.

I'd like to pick something up and hit him with it. "You know, this is the *last* thing I need right now, Carl—for you to be laying out all night doing no-telling-what with no-telling-who. I've got a lot on my plate, in case you haven't noticed, and I'm just about at the end of my rope. Can't you understand that?"

He grunts. "It ain't no cakewalk for me neither."

I snatch jeans and a T-shirt from a dresser drawer, then slam it shut. "How do I know you're telling the truth?

"You don't. But I am."

Standing at the foot of the bed, I stare down at him for a long time, until he starts snoring. I know this isn't the end of it, but for now the fight has gone out of me. I just can't deal with it, on top of everything else. I go into the bathroom and turn on the shower, reminding myself that no matter what happens, it's not worth getting so worked up about. But that's easier said than done.

***

Two weeks later, Daddy is much worse. I've missed a week of work to stay with him. For a few days, he was spitting up blood and complaining that his back hurt a lot worse, but as time went by, he stopped spitting or talking at all. The last thing he ate was half a can of chicken and stars, and that was four days ago, and he's not drinking water like he did either. Mostly, I keep his lips wet with a cloth. All of this is a natural progression, the hospice nurses tell me.

Every half hour, I check to make sure he's okay and wipe his face with a cold washcloth. Sometimes I just sit and look at him. He hasn't worn his dentures in years, so his nose and chin almost touch now, which puts me in mind of an old leprechaun, only there's nothing jolly about him. The nurses don't expect him to last much longer, and I know it's for the best that he doesn't, because otherwise he'll starve and just keep fighting to breathe.

When Saturday comes, I ask Carl to help me rake out the flower bed out front, just to get out in the sun for a few minutes and breathe a little fresh air before it gets so blazing hot, but he says he doesn't feel like it. I don't doubt that he doesn't, after drinking half a bottle of Jim Beam last night, and now all he wants to do is loll around on the couch and watch baseball. But he has been pretty nice lately, so I'm not going to say anything. He even helped me change Daddy's diapers last week, when Daddy was still eating and drinking a little, and he has cooked for us a few times, too.

I take a load of colors from the washer, put them in a basket, and tote them out to the clothesline. Mostly I use the dryer, but ever since I was a little girl, I've loved the smell of sun-dried clothes, especially sheets when you first crawl in them, so Carl put up the clothesline for me not long after we married.

I realize that I forgot the clothespins, so I set the basket on the grass and go back to get them.

He's at the kitchen table now, talking on the phone. "I'll talk to you later," he says and puts the phone down before I even get the door closed behind me.

"Who was that?"

He stands, hiking up his sweatpants, and lays back down on the couch. "Oh, it was Mama. I told her I'd try to get to that pump house tomorrow."

I take the bag of clothespins from the hook next to the washer and go back out, nearly tripping on the last porch step when my flip-flop catches on a nail. As I pin Carl's khaki pants to the line by the hems and pull out the pockets, I tell myself not to let my imagination get the best of me, but by the time I'm done hanging the clothes, I've imagined the worst: Carl has fallen for some floozy who looks at him like he's Tom Selleck, and our marriage is over. Just the idea of it makes me want to cry. But then, I'm not sure if he has done anything wrong.

I shut the door too hard when I go back in.

"What's the matter with you?" Carl says in a snippy tone.

I pass him without so much as a glance and head to the bathroom where I splash cold water on my face and take one of the nerve pills the doctor just prescribed me. Then I wet two clean washcloths, wring them out, and take them to Daddy's room. With one I gently wipe his face, and with the other I blot his parched lips, squeezing a few drops into his mouth.

I hate the thought of somebody needing water and can't get it.

ROSES

Stanley had gone to check the mail, and I was straining tea into a pitcher of sugar water, when I glimpsed it through the kitchen window: a big beige car with a dented door and rust patches the size of dinner plates, rolling down our street, bouncing slowly on its tires like a moon vehicle. Out by the mailbox, Stanley stopped shuffling the envelopes and stared, too. The car slowed as it grew closer, backfiring so loudly I almost dropped my boiler, the little red-handled, cast-iron one that had belonged to my mother. *Precious Lord,* I prayed, *please don't let that automobile stop where I'm afraid it's going to.* But my prayer failed me. The car pulled in next door, in front of the empty rental, its seats piled high with boxes.

The driver's door opened and out tumbled a little, white curly-haired dog that resembled a bedroom slipper. A sandy-haired girl in shorts and a sleeveless undershirt, the kind Stanley wore under his work shirts, only much tighter, got out, and she wasn't wearing a brassiere. More shocking than that, however, were the bandages on her forearms. I wondered if she had been in a wreck, but those were odd locations for injuries. The dog ran over to our wrought iron fence and squeezed into our yard.

The girl clapped at him. "Ozzy, you get back here!" But he was too busy sniffing my crepe myrtle to listen. "You come back here right now!" she said, stomping her foot, and just then the dog did his business, right there on Stanley's zoysia. "Oh Ozzy!" the girl wailed as she walked around the fence into our yard, her arms swinging. "I cannot believe you did that, you bad dog!"

Stanley stood with his hands on his hips. Tending to the lawn was how he spent the majority of his time, at least in the summer. I'd thought that when he retired, we would have the opportunity to do more things, maybe go see our son up in South Carolina or visit Gatlinburg, but he had only gotten busier and busier. Twice a week he mowed the grass, even if it didn't need it, trimming the edges two inches from the driveway and the curb. He had so many gadgets and chemicals, I didn't have nearly as much room for my gardening tools anymore, and still he bought more. But it was indeed a beautiful lawn.

The young woman scooped up the dog and started back to the rental. She said something to Stanley, but I couldn't make it out. He shook his head, and she said something else, then she carried the dog back to the car. Still clutching the animal, she pulled out a large black trash bag full of clothes or some other soft material, and toted them both to the front door. I stirred the tea until all of the sugar had dissolved, then I poured some over glasses of ice and set them on the table.

I dreaded Stanley's reaction to the house being occupied again. He would not be happy, though we knew it was inevitable. It had been vacant for four months, four months he had relished. The place had been a source of great displeasure to him since Mrs. Henley died three years ago and left it to her son. Stanley never dreamed the boy would turn it into a rental, something I'd heard him say at least twenty times, nor did I. We thought young Henley would sell it to a nice family, and that would be the end of it. But it wasn't to be. Stanley maintains that he did it for meanness, because of our magnolia limb falling onto his car one Fourth of July.

In spite of everything, we had excellent luck with the first tenants. They were exceptional really, a young couple with a baby. Stanley had liked them, too, because they were Southern Baptists and kept their grass mowed. In a way, the young lady reminded me of my daughter-in-law, the color of her hair perhaps, or something about the shape of her eyes, and she took an interest in my roses, which endeared her to me as well. Sometimes I'd pick small bouquets for her, and once, when her parents were visiting, I took a large arrangement in my best Lenox vase, which seemed to please her greatly. On the sad day when she left, I sent her off with a Mary Marshall miniature, something I reserved for my most cherished friends.

We were not so lucky with the next tenant, a young man with a motorcycle. At first he was quiet, in fact he was hardly ever home, and we congratulated ourselves on our good fortune, but then summer came, and he began to go around shirtless in the front yard and to have friends over who spent a great deal of time on the front porch, drinking and listening to raucous music. Once, when Stanley was edging the lawn, they offered him a beer. Stanley turned off the Weed Eater, pulled himself up straight, and announced without an ounce of shame, that the love of Jesus was far more intoxicating than alcohol, to which one of them replied "Well, if you'll put it in a can, I'll be glad to drink it," and they all had quite a laugh. Stanley was so angry he didn't sleep well for a week.

***

He threw the mail on the counter and sat down without speaking, and I joined him at the table. After he turned thanks, he shook open his napkin, and stuffed it into his collar. Pushing his glasses up the bridge of his nose with his little finger, he said, "Well, I reckon you see that we have a new neighbor."

I passed him the rice. "Yes, I saw that." I waited as he dipped some onto his plate, then I handed him the green beans. "She appears to have been in an accident."

"She appears to have a dog, too." He cut his pork chop into large pieces, put one in his mouth and chewed as he looked out the window. "I don't know where she thinks she'll keep it. The fence behind that place has completely rotted out."

I dipped a few beans onto my plate and cut one in half, thinking of the English setter Frankie had when he was a boy, though he had it for only a short time. He had been such a responsible pet owner, keeping the puppy clean and fed, and as soon as he got home from school each day, he played with him until dark. But before too long, the dog began to wreak havoc: digging up amaryllis bulbs and eating them; creating big holes between the magnolia roots, which caused a mess when it rained; and tearing his bed and anything else he could get his teeth on into a million pieces. He chewed up the garden hoses, and he even chewed a hole in the wall of the utility room, where he slept.

I tried my best to convince Stanley that it was only a stage, and the puppy would be a fine companion one day, but after a few more weeks of it, he loaded him into the back of his truck while Frankie was at school, and we never saw him again. I was as upset as our son when he got home and the dog wasn't there. I was certain that the incident, and perhaps a few others, were the reason he and his family seldom visited.

It wasn't that Stanley was heartless. He loved Frankie. He had been so proud that he got good marks and was the quarterback of the football team, and he worked hard at the gas company so Frankie could have nice clothes, go on class trips, and buy uniforms and sports equipment. He even bought him a car for his sixteenth birthday—not a fancy one, but it got him to school and to his part-time job, and allowed him to go on dates without borrowing ours. And Stanley was still as proud of him as ever, telling anyone who would listen that his son was a senior engineer for a big firm in Greenville. Still, I had never been sure if Frankie saw through Stanley's stern exterior, although I tried to explain to him that it was simply the way his father was raised.

"And did you see that car?" Stanley asked. "Now won't that be a mess, leaking oil all over the driveway?"

If there was another thing he couldn't abide, it was a car that wasn't taken care of. He was a firm believer in regular maintenance, driving our car to Underwood Auto on Main Street to have the oil changed regularly and to ensure that the filters and hoses were kept in proper working condition, which was why it ran like a sewing machine, though it was thirteen years old. Tim, the station owner, was always asking when Stanley was going to sell the car to him, which pleased Stanley immensely.

He drank some tea and took another bite of pork. "For forty years this has been a decent neighborhood, but it appears to be turning into a circus." He looked at me as if he expected a reply, his eyes magnified by his glasses, putting me in mind of a dragonfly. I tried to think of something encouraging to say, but nothing leapt to mind. He placed his knife across the top of his plate, pushed back his chair and stomped off.

I was still picking at my lunch when I heard the lawnmower start. I scraped the food from his plate onto mine and carried them both to the sink. The young woman was back outside, standing next to my Crimson Glory that grew along the fence. I set the plates on the counter, backed up a step, and watched her.

Bending, she cupped a rose in her hand and pulled it to her nose. I pulled the corner of my apron. If there was one thing that nettled me, it was someone dallying with my roses. Surely she wouldn't pick it, but you never knew about folks these days. Stanley says there's no limit to what they'll do. She closed her eyes and smelled it, then gazed at it for a few moments as she ran her fingers over the petals. Finally, she let go, and it fell back into its rightful position.

I untied my apron and hung it from a hook inside the pantry door. I hoped she wouldn't make a habit of handling my roses. Perhaps I should have said something. Stanley would have, had he seen her. He says if you give people an inch, they'll take Interstate Ten. But I supposed it didn't hurt a thing for her to smell one.

***

The next Sunday, Stanley went to get a new ceiling fan, and I was in the backyard mixing rose food when I heard a voice at the front of the house. "Hello? Hello?" I twisted the sprayer nozzle off and laid it on a bench, but before I could walk around to see who it was, the young woman appeared at the corner of the house. She wore a wrinkled yellow ankle-length dress, and she still wasn't wearing a brassiere, though she did have on shoes, sandals that hadn't been well cared for. She also had on a great deal of eyeshadow and lipstick that was quite dark and didn't suit her pale complexion.

She smiled, extending her hand, and with something of a jolt, I observed a small gold ring in her nose. "I'm Skyler Merchant," she said. "I just moved in next door."

I removed a glove and shook her hand. It was very cold. On her middle finger was a small star tattoo, and I couldn't help looking at the bandages on her arms. "Lila Pennfield."

"Nice to meet you, Mrs. Pennfield. Listen, I was wondering if I could use your cell. Mine's not working right now."

I nodded. "Yes, let me get it for you."

I was glad Stanley wasn't there. He wouldn't approve of me handing my phone to a stranger, but it wouldn't hurt anything just this once. I hung my hat by the back door, and she followed me into the den, wiping her feet just as I did. Taking the phone from a basket on the credenza, I gave it to her, then went to the kitchen and poured some apple juice, careful to stay within hearing range. I heard her say her refrigerator wasn't working, from which I surmised that she was speaking to the Henley boy. When she was through, she came into the kitchen.

"My fridge is on the blink, but the landlord says he'll send somebody over in the morning."

"Well, that's good news." She was silent while I sipped my juice. "Would you like some juice or maybe some tea?"

"Oh, no, thank you, I've got to get busy. I'm trying to get the house fixed up."

I followed her back into the yard, noticing a tear in the back of her dress, something I could have fixed in a jiffy. She thanked me for letting her use my phone, and at the corner of the house she stopped beside my Old Blush, the only China rose I had, and smiled. "You sure got some pretty roses."

"They are lovely, aren't they? June is their finest month." Just then, I caught a glimpse of our car coming down the street. "Well, it was nice to meet you, Skyler," I said, pulling on my gloves, but to my dismay, she stayed until Stanley drove up. He got out and glanced at me, but he didn't speak as he walked to the trunk and removed a big box. He sat it on the ground and nodded at her.

"Stanley, this is Skyler Merchant."

She stretched out her hand. "Nice to meet you, Mr. Pennfield. We spoke before, but now I know your name."

He shook her hand briefly. "Likewise," he mumbled, as he removed a receipt from his shirt pocket and began to scrutinize it.

"Well," she said, "It's nice to meet y'all. Thanks again, Mrs. Pennfield. You never know what's going to need fixing, and man, it's always something—not to mention the first month's rent plus deposit, and utility deposits, too... Jesus."

I looked at Stanley. "Oh, I'm sure it's costly alright," I said, wishing she would go home or he would go inside.

"I just moved here from Tennessee, but my boyfriend was born and raised here. We live together, but he works offshore, so he won't be home until next month."

Stanley picked up the box and gave me a look as I held the door for him. To my disappointment, he put it down and came right back out. Standing on the porch, he took his handkerchief from his shirt pocket and patted his face with it. "Young lady?" he said.

"Yes sir?"

"Are you familiar with our Lord and Savior Jesus Christ?"

She looked at her sandals. "Yes sir... a little."

"Well then, you ought to know that living with a man out of wedlock is a sin."

She looked at him for a long moment, but I detected no malice in her eyes. "Thanks again," she said to me, and as she walked away, I couldn't help noticing how prominent her shoulder blades were through the thin dress material.

I followed Stanley into the house and watched as he unfolded his pocket knife and lowered himself to his knees in front of the box. "I have half a mind to call that Henley boy," he said, slashing the cellophane, then he stopped, placed his hands on his thighs, and looked up at me. "Can you believe what this neighborhood is turning into, Lila? If we're not careful, we'll be surrounded by drug dealers and prostitutes... if we're not already."

I reached across the counter for the bouquet of roses I'd picked that morning and slid them to me. It made me nervous when Stanley got worked up. I rotated the vase, admiring the flowers. The colors were simply exquisite. Sunfires, they were—orange like a sunset or like flames at night.

***

Two days later, when we got home from church, we found one of Stanley's Better Boys on the driveway. It was laying there mangled, with tomatoes still clinging to it, and I felt a sharp pain in my forehead. He didn't say a word as he got out, walked over, and picked it up. Taking my purse from the seat, I followed him into the backyard where the other tomatoes grew, and we discovered three more scattered about, with only one left standing.

“Oh my,” I said. He kicked a pine cone with his dress shoe, then marched across the yard, unlocked the back door and went in. Rubbing my head, I followed.

He took off his suit jacket and threw it across our bed. “Do we have Henley’s number?”

“Not that I know of.” We hadn’t said five words to Mrs. Henley’s son in years. Stanley unclipped his tie and pitched it toward the chair by the chest of drawers, but it fell short and landed on the floor. “Stanley,” I said, picking it up, “what if the dog didn’t do it?”

He stopped untucking his shirt and glared at me. “What if the dog didn’t do it? What do you mean what if the dog didn’t do it, Lila? How many times have my tomatoes been dug up before?”

“Well, I guess they haven’t.”

I went into the bathroom and closed the door. I didn’t like it when he raised his voice. I sat on the toilet seat and listened to him thrashing around, dropping coins on the dresser instead of into his change jar and tossing his shoes into the closet. The only time he wasn’t neat was when he was angry. I took off my shoes and stockings and waited.

Finally he left the room, and I crept into the hallway, just in time to hear the front door slam so hard it shook the windows, which made my heart flutter uneasily. He was going over there, just as I feared. I peeked around the dining room curtain and watched him stamp across the yard, but I turned away before he reached the door. I didn’t want to see what would happen next. Stanley never was one to beat around the bush. I used to respect him for that.

Back in the bedroom, I changed into a house dress, and went to get lunch started. I was tying on my apron when he got back. He took the glass cleaner from under the sink and sprayed his bifocals, and I waited for him to tell me what happened, but he didn’t, so I asked.

“Mainly,” he said, tearing a paper towel from the roll, “I told her what her dog had done and that if it happened again, I’d call the pound.”

“What did she say?”

He held up the glasses, checking for smudges, then buffed them some more and put them back on. “She said she was sorry and kind of whimpered and teared up a little, which is a tactic I'm sure she's used once or twice in her life. Lord only knows the story behind that girl."

***

Three days later, Skyler Merchant came to the front door. She was holding a round terracotta object and a six-pack of tomato plants. She wasn't wearing makeup, and the circles under her eyes were as purple as eggplants. I fumbled with the handle of the storm door Stanley kept locked even in the daytime, trying to locate the tiny lever to unlock it. When I finally got it open, she handed me the plants. The bandages on her arms were badly in need of changing.

"I'm sorry about what happened," she said, and then she gave me the round object. It was the size of a salad plate, and it had a square hole in the middle and what looked like Chinese markings on it.

"Why thank you."

Before I could ask what it was, she said, "It's a Chinese coin. They had them at the dollar store. It didn't cost much."

"I see."

She smiled. "It's for good luck."

I set the plants on the porch swing and rotated the object in my hands, examining it. Four Chinese figures were imprinted in the clay, numbers I guessed. "What am I supposed to do with it?"

"Anything you want. I'm going to hang mine on the front door."

Stanley appeared in the doorway, watching through the glass. "What's that?" he asked.

"It's a Chinese coin, Stanley. It's meant to bring good luck. Wasn't that thoughtful of Skyler? And look, she brought you some tomato plants."

"I appreciate it, Miss," he said, "but I've already planted more tomatoes. Why don't you try your hand at growing them?"

"Oh," she said, "I'm no good at growing things."

He reached around the door and took the clay coin, glanced at it and handed it back to me. "That's a nice gesture, young lady, but we can't accept it. In this house we don't believe in luck. We believe in right living."

"Stanley!" I said, embarrassed. "Don't be rude!" But he just turned and walked away as if he hadn't said a thing.

Skyler took it from me and picked up the plants; then she stood on the edge of the porch, looking down the street. Before I could get enough wits about me to think of something to say, she left, and I stood there, watching her cross the yard, the TV blaring so loudly I could hear the weatherman forecasting rain.

***

The next day, although it was time to start dinner, I got my trimming shears and gloves, and studied the collection of vases on a shelf in the potting shed, trying to decide which one to use. I settled on a round one that held a delphinium arrangement my son sent last Mother's Day. It had been such a marvelous explosion of color, the delphiniums interspersed with spikes of scarlet salvia and a few Bells of Ireland. Each year I eagerly awaited the flowers he sent, wondering what breathtaking composition would appear next. For a few minutes I stood in the dim shed, enjoying the peace and the smell of potting soil as I admired the vase. The deep blue color reminded me of my mother's eyes.

Donning my work apron, I headed to my Betty Prior at the corner of the porch. It was full of flowers, and I began to snip them, perhaps more aggressively than I should have, though still careful to cut the stems at an angle so they could drink. Before long, I had a large bouquet. I filled the vase at the spigot by the shed and arranged them informally, the way that suited them best.

Out of the corner of my eye, I glimpsed my Ivory Fashion topiary, which was truly a sight to behold, so full of blooms that it looked like a fluffy little cloud on a stalk. Just to see it brought cheer to my heart. I had planted another one in a small pot on the porch, but it was yet too young to train. With resolve, I went over and picked it up, and carrying both, I headed next door.

I ascended the steps carefully, avoiding raised nails and splinters in the old wood. It was the first time I'd been there since the young couple had moved, and I was surprised that it was in such disrepair. Mr. and Mrs. Henley would never have allowed it, nor the young couple. A small wreath covered in plastic sunflowers hung on the door, the Chinese coin above it. Setting the pot near my feet and cradling the vase of roses, I rapped on the door.

Skyler cracked it open and peeked out, still in pajamas that late in the day. Her dog bounced around her feet, trying to squeeze through her legs, but she gently pushed him back with her foot. The bandages on her arms had been changed. She looked at the roses and then at me.

"I want to apologize for my husband's behavior," I said. "He's just... well, he's just a little overzealous at times, I guess you could say."

She smiled a little. "Oh, that's all right."

I held out the roses. "I thought you might enjoy these. They're Betty Priors.

She came out and took them, then raised them to her face. "Thank you, Mrs. Pennfield. It's sweet of you to bring them."

I picked up the pot. "I'd also like to give you this small one. It's called an Ivory Fashion.

She shook her head. "No ma'am. I don't mean to be rude, but no. I'd kill it in a week."

"Well, you just keep it and see," I said, patting her hand. "If it starts looking poorly, I'll help you with it." I placed it on the left side of the porch where it could get morning sun, out of the shade of her Chinaberry. On my way down the steps, I stopped and looked back at her. "I'll tell you a little secret about roses," I said with a wink. "They know if you love them, and if you do, they'll love you back."

***

That evening while we were eating supper, we watched as Skyler dragged a wooden chair with a faded aqua seat across the grass between her house and ours, the dog tromping around her feet. She stopped at her kitchen window, over which she had draped a pink striped sheet as a curtain, and positioned the chair beneath it. She left for a few minutes then returned with a hammer in one hand and a horseshoe in the other. Scrambling onto the chair, seemingly unbothered by its wobbling, she stood on her tiptoes, pounded a nail and hung the horseshoe.

Stanley stopped buttering his corn, his knife poised, watching her. She climbed down and waved at us. I smiled and waved back, and she disappeared around the house. He put down the knife. "I wonder if it's too much to ask that we be allowed to eat in peace, without being stared at like monkeys in a zoo."

The horseshoe brought back a memory of one my father nailed over our barn door when I was a child. It had belonged to Goldie, the little horse he bought for me at the auction in Dothan. I loved her more than anything and spent every spare minute with her that I could. Sometimes she would pull at my dress when she wanted a treat, and I'd feed her loose sugar from my hand, since we didn't have sugar cubes, delighting in her soft mouth against my palm. I could see her plainly, standing under her little shed, hay rolled up in the field behind her.

***

It happened on a Wednesday morning, about a week after I'd last talked to Skyler Merchant. It was just a matter of time, I supposed. If her little dog hadn't chewed one of Stanley's sprinkler heads, he would have chewed or dug up something else. We didn't see him much, but the poor thing had to get out sometime. I had gone to take a sweet potato pie to Mrs. Weaver, a widow down the street, and I was away for only five or ten minutes when I heard the commotion.

"Well, what in the world!" I said, handing the pie to her through the front door and hurrying back to the house.

Stanley and Skyler Merchant were shouting at each other across the fence, Stanley waving his arms like a windmill in a hurricane, and Skyler shifting her dog from one hip to the other, screaming, "I'll buy you another stupid sprinkler head!" over and over.

"You're going to do more than that, young lady!" he said, jabbing the air with his finger. "You're going to get rid of that dog!"

Before I could reach them, he huffed into the house, the door slamming behind him, and she strode angrily to her door. Just before going in, she yelled, "Who do you think you are, God or something?"

I didn't see the animal control truck drive up later, but I heard Stanley talking. Peering through the kitchen window, I saw a young man with a leash in his hand. I quietly raised the window and heard him tell Stanley that he didn't want to take the dog, that maybe he could get the owner to put up a temporary fence or something, but Stanley wouldn't have it. He told him that he was an old man on a fixed income, and he couldn't afford to have his garden ripped up and his sprinkler heads ruined, then he asked about his "good friend" Mr. Dodd, the county commissioner. Eventually, the man gave in. He said that if the dog didn't have his shots, he would take him. I went into the bathroom, closed the door, and wept.

***

For the next two weeks, I kept an eye out for the dog, but I never saw him. I was sure that the animal control people charged a handsome fee, but I felt certain that Skyler would retrieve him if she could afford it. I had not seen her either, though her car was there, and the kitchen light came on at night. After mulling it over for a while, and taking into account that I might not be welcome, I decided to bake her a cake and offer to pay her dog-related expenses.

On her porch, I noticed that the rose I'd given her was nearly dead from lack of water. Maybe I'd come back and give it a drink, I told myself, though I feared it had already gone up the spout. Softly, I knocked on the door. I waited a few moments, but when there was no answer and no sound of anyone approaching, I knocked a little louder. I tried a third time, and just as I was about to leave, her face appeared in the window. She blinked as if she'd been sleeping, then slowly opened the door.

She looked so dreadful, I was afraid she could see the shock on my face. Her cheeks were hollow, and her hair looked as if it hadn't been brushed in a week. She wore a green rayon robe, tied in a tight knot at the waist, and she smelled of cigarette smoke. "Hi," she said, barely above a whisper.

"I haven't seen you in a while. Have you been ill?"

"Yes Ma'am. I think the flu or something."

"I'm sure sorry to hear that," I said. "I hope you won't be offended, Skyler, but I'd like to pay any fees that are required to get your little dog back."

"Oh, thank you, but my boyfriend sent the money. I got him out, plus all of his shots and everything. My boyfriend's mother is keeping him for now."

"That's wonderful." I was happy to hear that the dog was safe. "Is your boyfriend going to make it home before long?" I asked, adding that I didn't mean to pry. "I'm sure you miss him."

"Yes ma'am, I do. But he works a whole lot of overtime."

"Well, I guess that's a good thing." I held out the cake. "I brought you a red velvet. I don't know of anyone who doesn't like them."

"Aw, that's nice of you."

She stepped through the door, and as she reached for the cake, she dropped her phone. When she kneeled to pick it up, her robe fell open around her legs, and I couldn't keep from gasping. There were cuts in many places, mostly on her lower legs, some partially healed and some more recent, raw and rather deep in places. I quickly looked away before she saw me staring, but she didn't seem to notice. She stood and took the cake from me.

Gathering my composure, I said, "Well, I'll let you get your rest now. Should you need anything at all, please let me know."

She blew her bangs from her eyes. "Thanks, Mrs. Pennfield. I appreciate that." And then she closed the door.

***

The digital clock on the dresser read 12:40 a.m. as red lights sliced through our bedroom. I bolted upright, my heart racing, hearing muffled voices outside. Stanley was nowhere to be seen. Scooting to the edge of the bed, I stepped into my slippers and hurried down the hall. I found him on the front porch looking over at the rental. An ambulance was parked next to Skyler Merchant's car, its lights pulsing crimson, while a police car sat beside it and a woman in uniform spoke into a device. Someone answered, but the static made it hard to decipher.

Suddenly, the front door of the house flew open, and two men in orange shirts rushed out carrying someone on a stretcher with an arm dangling over the side. They trotted to the back of the ambulance and climbed in with it, the woman quickly closing the doors behind them, then she jumped into the driver's seat and they sped away, the siren wailing.

The policeman walked over with a clipboard. "Do you folks know that girl?"

I told him her name. "Is she all right?"

"Not sure. Do you know if she has family around here?"

"No, she's from Tennessee," I said, "but her boyfriend is from here, though we've never met him."

"We don't know what his name is," Stanley added.

The man nodded. "Well, thanks. You folks have a good night." We watched him return to his car and drive away.

"We need to get in touch with that Henley boy, and let him know what's gone on over there," Stanley said.

I could see the potted rose in the pale porch light, and the wreath and coin on her door. "She'll be back," I said.

He swiveled his head sharply to look at me. "What makes you think so?" His hair stood like stiff bristles—his lips were pursed in disapproval.

"Because I feel it in my heart, Stanley. And because I'm praying for it."

He stared at me for a few moments, then he shook his head and opened the door. "Remind me to spray some WD-40 on those hinges tomorrow," he said, holding it open for me.

"I'm not going in just yet."

He raised his eyebrows, then shrugged. "Suit yourself." And he closed the door behind him.

The moon was full, and my Natchez crepe myrtle blossoms stood out from the shadows like specters. Next door, the moonlight etched Skyler Merchant's old beige car, and beside it, along the fence, my Crimson Glory, laden with roses, drooped toward the ground, burdened by its own weight.

DOTTIE'S LIFE

When I was a little girl, I used to daydream that my father was dead. I'd sit in the trees and think about it. I'd lie awake at night and think about it. I thought about it on the playground. I'd imagine my teacher asking if my father could help drive the class to the USS Alabama on our field trip, to which I'd reply with my head hanging low, "I'm sorry, ma'am, but he was killed in a terrible car crash," or "He stepped on a landmine in Vietnam," or "He died from an inoperable brain tumor." But I knew that anyone could read the truth like Morse code in my blinking, fibbing eyes: he just didn't care enough to hang around.

The person I envied most was my cousin, Dottie. And not just because she had a father, lots of people had them, but because she had the best one in the world, my Uncle J.W. He doted on her, took her to live in places like Texas and the Philippines, places I'd only stuck pushpins into on a map, bought her anything she wanted: tape players and Barbies and bright knit shirts and bell-bottoms like the teenagers wore, with matching daisy ponytail holders to twist her long dark hair into.

The fact that she was diabetic and took two shots a day only made him more affectionate. Everybody worried about her. When her name came up, the grown-ups paid attention. Sometimes, lying on the sparse grass out by the pump house, watching the pine tops brush the sky, I'd wish that I was diabetic, too. Even the shots would be worth it, I figured. They couldn't hurt all that much, not in the thigh. I wouldn't even mind going into a coma like she did once either. How bad could it be to dream away, while everyone stood around your hospital bed fretting? Even my father might come.

Next to Dottie, I was very aware that my teeth were crooked and my clothes secondhand, but even so, I felt redeemed in her presence, uplifted, a part of the world "out there." I wanted to be different, a different girl in a different place, far away from Rock Creek, the middle of nowhere Alabama, where old men thought the Beatles were part of a communist plot, and that Neil Armstrong didn't actually walk on the moon—that it was trick photography or a staged set. I hated my life. And that was especially true in 1969, the summer I went to Georgia with Dottie.

I was going through a confusing time then, a time when I'd begun to question my self-worth. I must not be a good girl or my father would love me. His absence hadn't bothered me so much before. My parents had divorced when I was six, so I was used to it. Maybe it was school the past year, and the first time I'd really noticed that other kids had daddies who helped with the hayrides at the Halloween carnival or came to watch the competitions on Field Day. But most likely it was because I'd seen him for the first time since he had driven us to my grandparent's house and left us, three years earlier.

It was the beginning of August, and my brother and I had ridden our bikes to the country store, a half mile from where we lived. My brother had already started home, having grown impatient while I chose what to buy with my 35 cents. I was about to push up my kickstand when the car drove up, a big shiny blue one that I hadn't seen around, and a woman was sitting close to the man who was driving. Stuffing bubblegum into my mouth, I waited to see who it was. After all, there were only about fifty people in Rock Creek, and I knew every one of them. The car made a big circle and parked.

When I realized who was driving, I just stood there frozen, holding my grape drink and bag of candy in one hand and gripping the handlebar with the other, unable to decide what to do. I didn't know if I should hop on my bike and pedal fast or stay put. I wished my brother hadn't left, but he was already out of sight.

My father tipped his ball cap to the old men on the bench in front of the store. "How are you fellas?"

The woman in the car played with a string of beads that hung from the rearview mirror. One of the old men looked at me, and then so did my father.

I couldn't decipher the expression on his face when he saw me. I couldn't tell what he thought. I gazed down at my feet, embarrassed. My big toe was bleeding on top, where I'd stumped it against the pavement.

"Well, hey, little gal," he said. "Ain't you gonna give your daddy a hug?" He strolled over and embraced me, making me spill some of my drink. He smelled kind of like Granny's spice drawer, and I liked it a lot. I wondered if I should kiss him like I kissed Mama and my brother and sister, but I decided against it. He might not like that kind of thing. Over his shoulder, the woman in the car was staring.

"So what are you up to?" he asked.

"I was just getting a drink."

"Grape, huh?"

I nodded, squinting up at him, shielding my eyes from the sun with my hand.

He looked away, down the blacktop toward Bradley, and I decided that he was the handsomest man I ever saw, and it made me proud. His eyes were green like mine, and his hair was almost the color of mine, too, only a little darker. He had a V-shaped scar on his chin, but it wasn't big enough to notice much, and he wore a T-shirt with the sleeves rolled up, showing strong arms. I took it all in, even his fingernails, so I could remember it later.

"How's your brother and sister?" he asked.

"Fine."

A drop of water trickled down my bottle and splatted the asphalt, spreading to the size of a quarter. I waited for him to say something else, but he didn't. I don't know what I expected him to say: "I'm sorry I haven't seen you for so long, but my legs were paralyzed, and I couldn't get to you, though I tried," or "I've missed you so much you wouldn't believe it, and everything, from this moment on, will be different"?

He reached into his back pocket and took out an old brown billfold from which he removed fifteen dollars, a ten and five ones, and handed them to me. "Five for you and five for your brother and sister," he said, then he tousled my hair. “Well, gal, I’ve got to get going. You take care of yourself, okay?”

“Yes sir,” I said, as he turned and walked away.

“I’ll be there in a minute,” he called to the woman, and he went into the store, the screen door slapping behind him.

***

When I went home with Dottie two weeks later, it was the first time I’d ever been out of Alabama, and going to another state, even a neighboring one, was like going to Neptune. Uncle J.W. had just been stationed at Robins Air Force Base, and they had come home to see Aunt Gwen’s mother, who had rheumatoid arthritis and wasn’t doing well. “Why don’t you let Jackie come home with us?” Aunt Gwen asked Mama. I’d been shocked and thrilled at the same time.

“Well, I don’t know. She’s never been away from home.”

“Please,” I begged.

“We’ll be back to see Mother in a week, Kathleen,” Aunt Gwen said. “Let her go with us.”

We left at night, just as the moon was rising like a big orange in the sky. The Plymouth Valiant was running hot, Uncle J.W. said, and the night would be easier on it. After climbing into the back with Dottie, I watched him walk up our rickety steps, to where Mama stood in the porch light, and hand her some money. She shook her head but he took her hand and put it in it, then she hugged him, and he jumped off the porch and slid behind the wheel.

I looked back as we drove away, at Mama waving on the porch and my brother and sister watching through the screen door, and for a minute I was afraid to leave the people who loved me most. But by the time we rounded the first curve, my sense of adventure won out, and I was elated at the thought of going to a whole other state. I was happy to be included in a family that had been to so many places and took it all for granted, like it was no more than walking to the refrigerator or to the mailbox across the road. That’s how I would act, too, when I got back home, I decided. I wouldn’t brag.

We drove through the Conecuh Forest, and in thirty minutes we were in Brewton, where I was born. I couldn't wait to get through town, because after that, everything would be new. Uncle J.W. reached back and handed me a map, then he turned on the overhead light.

I traced my finger up the squiggly line that would lead us to Georgia, with names of towns written on either side of it, names like Fort Deposit and Letohatchee, places I'd never heard of. After he turned off the light, I closed my eyes and imagined them, full of stores and churches and schools where people were born and worked and lived and maybe died without ever getting to go anywhere else.

When we passed the county line, Uncle J.W. took a thin, flat bottle from the glove compartment, unscrewed the cap, and drank from it. I didn't know for sure if it was whiskey, but I suspected it was, because I had heard Granny praying about him once when she didn't know anybody was in the house. I watched him drink, admiring the way the bottle glinted in the pale light of the dashboard. A strong, sweet smell filled the car. Aunt Gwen looked at him for a long time, and Dottie looked out the window. He screwed the cap back on and wiped his mouth on the back of his hand, just like in a western.

Uncle J.W. was a small man with a big personality. He was proud and a little showy, and I liked him. He had spent a long time in Vietnam, Mama said, where it was his job to identify dead airmen and tell their families. I tried to picture it, conjuring up images of him in his uniform, holding his hat in his hand, knocking on a door that would be opened by parents who looked like Timmy's parents on the old Lassie reruns, and he would tell them the sad news, and then the mother would bury her face in her husband's chest and cry. Uncle J.W. would let them know that their son was very brave, and they would all go inside and talk and drink coffee for a long time, and by the time he left, they would feel better.

He stuffed the bottle under the seat and said, "Let's sing something. You girls pick one."

Dottie pulled the door lock up and down. "My Favorite Things" sprang to mind and the kookaburra song I'd learned in school, but those were too silly to mention, so I said I couldn't think of anything.

Taking Aunt Gwen's hand, he said, "Let's sing 'Harbor Lights.'"

It was a song I'd never heard on the top forty station out of Pensacola, but it was my uncle's favorite, I learned later, a song that reminded him of San Diego, where he'd done a stint in the navy before he joined the air force.

He sang by himself mostly, with Aunt Gwen joining in on the chorus. He had a beautiful voice, rich and smooth, and I smiled at Dottie and rested my head on the back of the seat, listening. It was a sad song about loving someone who went away.

After that, Aunt Gwen suggested "Bye Bye Blackbird," which I could easily sing along to. Occasionally she would turn around and wink at us, then turn back again, her head swaying as she sang, her thick dark hair falling to her shoulders in loose waves. Aunt Rennie said she never could see what men saw in Aunt Gwen. She said her eyes were too big, and she looked like a deer right in the face, but I knew she was just jealous. Aunt Gwen was dainty and elegant like Audrey Hepburn, and she wore cigarette pants that tapered just above her ankles and jewel-studded gold sandals like an Arabian princess. Sometimes she wore her hair in a ponytail with a bandana tied around it, and she looked just like a teenager. I smiled, watching her smoke her cigarette, her arm draped over the back of the seat, her graceful hand resting on Uncle J.W.'s shoulder.

After a few more songs, I fell asleep and didn't wake up until after midnight. We were at a gas station, and Uncle J.W. was pumping gas and checking the radiator. We went inside, and Aunt Gwen bought me a Pepsi and Dottie a Tab, and she gave us each a yellow apple out of a bag in the trunk. Then we drove on through the night. Before too long, we passed a sign that said "Welcome to Georgia," which was exciting, although the scenery didn't look any different from Alabama, as far as I could tell in the moonlight—just more fields and pine trees.

"Let's sing another one," said Uncle J.W, his words slurring just a little.

Aunt Gwen gave him another long look. "Why don't you let me drive for a while?"

He leaned forward and adjusted his seat. "I'm fine, Gwen. Why don't you quit worrying all the time?" Dottie turned to the window and so did Aunt Gwen.

"We're here, girls," my aunt said, and I woke up in time to see us entering the gate to the base. The guard, in his shiny black shoes and tilted hat, reminded me of "The Nutcracker" I'd seen on TV last Christmas. He waved us through with a gloved hand, and we entered a world of gray and beige buildings and signs labeled "support," and "command," and "commissary."

Half-asleep, we walked through the front door, into the smell of lemon oil and floor wax, and Aunt Gwen switched on the light, revealing dark wooden furniture with olive green cushions and a heavy gold mirror above the couch. On one side of the mirror was a portrait of a Spanish man, and on the other, a Spanish woman with black lace draped over her face. A gigantic wooden spoon and fork hung over the dining room table which held a bowl of wooden fruit. Uncle J.W. kissed us goodnight, and I followed Dottie down the hall to her bedroom. I knew beyond a shadow of a doubt that she was the luckiest girl ever.

When I opened my eyes the next morning, I didn't know where I was for a few seconds, but then I remembered, and I was filled with wonder as I took in the lacy pink curtains and bedspread and the pink sheets trimmed with ruffles. Stuffed animals were everywhere, and also big baby dolls and games stacked on a large white shelf. The sun streamed in like Hollywood lights. It was the most glorious room I had ever seen.

Next to me, Dottie opened her eyes and smiled. "I'm glad you're here," she said.

We ate cereal in the kitchen, then sat on the couch watching TV while Aunt Gwen vacuumed and dusted and ironed embroidered lace pillowcases and slips and doilies. The air conditioning was so nice, I felt sleepy again.

"Let's go play in my room," Dottie said, so I followed her back down the hall. Closing the door, she pointed to the big furry rug on the floor. "We can sit there."

I sat, wondering what we were going to play, when she opened the closet and slid out the biggest Barbie Dreamhouse I'd ever laid my eyes on. I'd seen them at Kmart, but they weren't nearly as fabulous as this one. It must have been the most expensive one they made. She dragged it to the rug, then she went back to the closet and pulled out a Barbie convertible and a clear carrying case full of Barbies, Kens, Midges, and Skippers. I held my breath as she unlocked the Dreamhouse and opened it.

It was lovely beyond description, a piece of pure heaven, and I scooted closer and stared, enchanted. I wanted to take all of it in my arms, but I waited respectfully for Dottie to choose the doll she wanted, then I selected mine, a brunette Barbie with green eyes. Next, I began the slow, thoughtful process of selecting an outfit from the overstuffed dream closet. There was so much to choose from: mod, flowered mini dresses and bright, ruffled blouses, all manner of ball gowns made of lace and satin, with high heels to match. There were fluffy bedroom shoes and round suitcases with Barbie's face on them, and even a little white dog with a red collar. There was a picnic table with a checkered cloth and a tiny basket full of plates and glasses, a hair dryer for Barbie to sit under, and so much more.

I scaled my thoughts to Barbie size and dressed my doll for a ball, pampering her at the little pink vanity, chatting with Dottie's blonde Barbie about what the night would bring: dancing and romance under the stars. In their world there was nothing else to think about. They weren't the least bit concerned about lunch money or outgrowing their shoes or making things easier for a mother who cried herself to sleep. The only things they had to think about were parties and picnics and the beach and what to wear to them.

The next evening, Aunt Gwen was peeling potatoes for supper when Uncle J.W. came home. Dottie and I were working on a jigsaw puzzle on the card table that Aunt Gwen had set up by the dining room window. He walked over and looked at the puzzle, nodding approval. It was a red barn in a field of different colored flowers, but we had put together only the outline and a little more in the bottom right corner. "And how are you two lovely girls this evening?" he said, bending to kiss Dottie's forehead and then mine.

"We're fine," I answered.

Dottie rummaged through the pieces and didn't say anything.

"Don't set a place for me, Gwen," he said, walking over to kiss her cheek. "I've got to head back to the office and finish some paperwork, then I'm going to swing by the NCO club and have a beer with Frank Mitchell. You know he's retiring tomorrow."

She took the bowl of potatoes to the sink, and he followed her, putting his arms around her waist and kissing her neck.

"I won't be long. I promise."

She twisted out of his arms and lifted a lid from a boiler on the stove, stirred the contents, and slammed the lid back down. Dottie picked up a puzzle piece and tried to make it fit where it wouldn't go, pushing so hard she bent it.

He leaned against the counter and sighed. "Gwen, I go to the club to relax a little with the guys. That's all I'm doing."

She wiped her hands on the dish towel and threw it on the counter. "Yes, and I go to the trouble of making your supper, and the least you can do is be here to eat it." Turning to Dottie and me, she said, "You girls go watch TV until it's ready."

Dottie groaned, got up, and went to the living room with me at her heels. Walter Cronkite was talking about all he ever talked about—Vietnam—as tired-looking soldiers with muddy faces tramped down a dirt road, their rifles slung across their backs.

"You said you were going to stop this, James," Aunt Gwen said in the kitchen. "First it's one drink at the club, and then it's another and another, and Lord only knows what else. I told you before... I won't live like this."

Dottie turned up the TV, but I could still hear the front door slam.

Sometime in the middle of the night, I woke to a crashing sound down the hall. It sounded like somebody had turned over the table or dropped something heavy on the floor. Dottie and I sat up and listened as the bathroom faucet came on and a door banged shut.

"All you ever do is badger me!" Uncle J.W. yelled. "You're nothing but a goddamned nag!" Aunt Gwen said something I couldn't make out, and he said, "Oh you think so? Well, I wouldn't count on it!"

Dottie's brown eyes glistened in the street light that shone dimly through the sheers. I thought I heard Aunt Gwen crying.

Before long, Uncle J.W. came bumping down the hall. "Pretend you're asleep!" Dottie whispered, pulling the covers to her neck.

He stopped at our door and eased it open, and through my barely open eyes I saw him stick his head in. He leaned over the bed and looked down at us for a few seconds. Dottie lay very still and so did I, trying to breathe like I was asleep. He reached down and snugged the covers around our necks, then he bent down and kissed Dottie's cheek.

"You'll wake them!" Aunt Gwen hissed from the hallway.

He wobbled out, and when I heard their bedroom door close, I propped my head on my elbow and looked at Dottie. "Is he like that a lot?"

"No," she said, wiping her eyes. "Not all the time."

When we got up the next morning, he had gone to work and Aunt Gwen was asleep on the couch. She blinked at us and sat up, tightening the belt of her silky white robe. "Morning," she muttered. "How did y'all sleep?"

"We slept okay," said Dottie.

"Y'all want to watch TV?"

She went into the kitchen and fixed toast and marmalade, diabetic marmalade that didn't taste very good, and Dottie and I ate, sitting cross-legged on the floor in our pajamas, watching a rerun of Gilligan's Island. When it ended, a cooking show came on, and we carried our plates to the kitchen where Aunt Gwen was drinking coffee at the table, staring out the window. We went back to the living room and Dottie slumped onto the couch.

"Want to play Barbies?" I asked.

She shrugged. "I guess."

In her room, she sat on the rug and told me I could get the Dreamhouse out if I liked. I felt honored that she would let me, so I was especially careful when I took it from her closet, unlatched it, and drew the halves apart. It was the only time I had opened it myself, and I pretended it was mine. "Which doll would you like?" I asked.

"I don't care."

That meant that I could pick the newest Barbie, but I didn't. Instead, I handed it to her. I got a Midge and began to dress her in a blue dress with a matching raincoat, gently removing them from their tiny hangers, while Dottie twirled Barbie's long blond hair around her finger. "You want me to choose an outfit for you?" I asked.

"If you want."

It wasn't hard to choose. I plucked the prettiest ball gown of all from the closet, a crimson velvety one trimmed in white fur, and held it out to her. She took it and dressed her Barbie, but she didn't act like her heart was in it. When I got my Midge done, I put her in the convertible with Ken and rolled them around the floor. *Where are they going?* I wondered. I decided that they were on their way to visit her parents who live in

Hollywood in a mansion with a swimming pool shaped like a heart and a garden full of Johnny-jump-ups, azaleas and pink roses. And a poodle. They had horses, too, named Black Beauty and Flicka, that would come running when Midge whistled. After a dinner of caviar and baked Alaska, Midge and Ken would go for a swim and then take a stroll in the moonlight.

Aunt Gwen appeared in the doorway, startling me. Embarrassed, I stopped the car and smiled up at her. She smiled back but her eyes looked sad. Picking up a tiny comb, I ran it through Midge's red hair as Dottie stared at her doll, not doing anything. "You girls play as long as you want," Aunt Gwen said. "I'm going to lie back down for a little while."

When she left, Dottie set the Barbie on the floor and climbed on the bed.

"Want me to put everything up?" I asked.

"No, go ahead and play if you want."

In the living room, the grandfather clock chimed ten times. I leaned back against the bedpost, wishing I could think of something to cheer her up, but if Barbies couldn't do it, I didn't know what could. Her life wasn't as easy as I thought. For one thing, being diabetic was a lot worse than I had guessed. Sometimes when Aunt Gwen gave her a shot, Dottie cried, and the shots left bruises on her legs, too. It would be awful, I concluded, to go to sleep every night, knowing that you had to get up and take another one the next morning and then a second one later in the day. And Dottie couldn't eat all the things I could. She had to have special candy and cookies, and they didn't taste good at all.

But more than anything, she didn't have the kind of daddy I believed she had. Not the kind we both wanted—the kind that took time for her and held her hand and snuggled her against him in the evenings, where she could breathe in the smell of him and feel safe. She had the kind of father you couldn't predict, the sort who could fly out of control and say things that hurt people, the kind who was too full of sad memories to tell her about the happy ones. I put the dolls back in their case, closed the Dreamhouse, and put it away.

***

Uncle J.W. and Aunt Gwen didn't argue again while I was there, even though he still left some nights after supper and didn't come home until we were asleep. His presence was mostly a voice in their bedroom late at night, and beyond that, I didn't see much more of him, until they drove me home.

Two years later, he and Aunt Gwen divorced, and a few years after that, she was diagnosed with rheumatoid arthritis, like her mother. I didn't see her again, but I heard that she started drinking and put on weight, and that she and her new husband didn't get along. I heard that the neighbors found her passed out once on the grass under the sprinklers.

Dottie got married right out of high school to a guy Uncle J.W. didn't like and moved to Louisiana, where he worked offshore, on an oil rig. "She could have done better," Uncle J.W. often said. "She could've made something of herself."

And my uncle drank until it killed him at sixty-seven. On the evening he passed away, I was crossing the Coronado Bridge into San Diego. The lights were coruscating across the bay below, and in the silence of the car, I could hear him singing "Harbour Lights" one last time.

As for my own father, I contacted him ten years ago, and I meet him for lunch if I'm home, usually at Christmas. I give him a wallet or a shirt, and he gives me chocolate-covered cherries and a card I know my stepmother—who is younger than me—picked out. "Come visit us in California," I say, and he always says he might just do that one day. Once in a while we talk on the phone, but the conversations are brief and typically consist of him telling me how much it has rained, always too much or too little, or what his stepkids are up to. Sometimes, in the background, I can hear them calling him Daddy.

THE SOYBEAN FIELD

Daddy threw his phone down so hard it was a wonder it didn't crack the screen. He jumped up and stomped into the living room, leaving me and my stepmother staring at each other across the table. Donnie Ebersole had called to tell him that the cows were back in the soybeans. It had been over a week since we'd run them out of the field, and we had started to believe that it was the last time we'd have to.

At the end of the table, his plate of catfish and hushpuppies was getting cold, and it made me feel bad for Francine, since she had already held off cooking until 7:30, waiting for us to get back from the farm supply in Dothan. She rubbed her fingers up and down her temples like she does when she's getting one of her headaches, and she started to say something, but we heard Daddy coming back, so we hushed up.

He came in toting his boots and sat, then pulled one on. "Five times," he said, spreading his fingers in her face, "five times that bastard's told me he'd take care of them cows, and five times he hasn't done it." He jerked on the other boot, got up, and plucked his John Deere cap from a hook by the door. "You see what a rich man's word is, don't you, Francine?" Yanking open the kitchen door, he said, "Come on, Jeff." I crammed two hushpuppies and the tail of a catfish into my mouth and caught up with him at the truck.

Dust churned in the high beams as we drove out of the yard and onto the dirt road that led to the two-lane blacktop. When we reached it, we turned right and wound through the woods toward the old Blackburn place—a rented seventy-acre plot that we'd planted in soybeans.

"Hand me that bottle," he said, so I plunged my hand under the seat, tapping the gritty floor until I touched glass. He grabbed it, twisted off the cap, and took a long swallow. The smell of Southern Comfort filled the cab.

Without a moon to light them, the woods were Bible-black, and it made me shiver in spite of the July heat that snugged around me like a quilt. I knew how lonely it was out in those pines, how deep into them, you could hear the wind whisper strange things, and you could feel the ghosts of the Muscogee. I gnawed my thumbnail and looked straight ahead, at the lights pushing the night from the road. In the shadows, Daddy's face was pale and his jaw muscles were flexing—a sure sign that he was pissed. He pulled a pouch of Red Man from his shirt pocket, packed a wad into his mouth, and chewed it hard and fast.

I looked down at my tennis shoes, my birthday present, wishing I'd had a chance to change into my boots. I wanted to keep them nice, because Daddy had shelled out a lot of money for them. It made me want to do things for him, too, like feed and water the bird dogs so he didn't have to, and keep the combine and the tractor clean and the lawnmower blade sharpened without being told. And it made me want to punch that old man Paxton right in the gut.

Daddy had every right to be mad. He'd had a bellyful of being jerked around by that old codger who thought he could walk all over anybody that didn't have money. I'd heard him on the phone with Mr. Paxton a couple of times, as polite as a man could be, calling him "sir" and "mister" and all that. "I wouldn't bother you, Mr Paxton, sir," he'd say, "but you know farming is hard work, sir, and I just can't afford to let them cows trample all over my crop." Over and over he said he'd send somebody to take care of it first thing in the morning, but over and over, he never did.

We'd tried everything to keep them out of the field. We'd fix the fence where they'd get in, but they would just find another sagging spot, and there we'd go again, riding out at all hours to chase them out of there. Of course, the whole fence needed replacing, but Daddy said we didn't have the time or the money to do it right now. Once, we even tried putting hay outside it so they would eat that instead, but they went through it in no time, and Daddy said he damn sure wasn't going to keep hauling hay to somebody else's cows. The last time we had to run them out of there, he had fired a few shots in the air, which at least made them pick up their pace and trot off, instead of gallivant away like usual.

It was plain that old man Paxton didn't give a rip about those cows. He probably had so many he couldn't keep track of them anyway, and they were just a few he stuck on some of his thousands of acres and forgot about. Lots of times I had driven by his place in town, a big Roman-looking mansion with azalea bushes and magnolias and a yard mowed down to a nub. What did somebody like him have to worry about? Why should he bother with a handful of cows?

All the same, it looked like he would care if they starved to death, which is what they were doing for a long time. When we first saw them, before we ever planted the field, their ribs stuck out like the ribs of those African kids on TV, with haunches so lean it made you wonder how they had the strength to stand up. I hated to see such as that, because they didn't know any better. Anybody knows that cows don't know diddly about fending for themselves. They're the tamest things there is. Course, they were faring a whole lot better since they found the beans.

We turned off the road and rattled down a rough, narrow one, across Yellow Creek bridge, and on farther into the woods, until we finally stopped at the gate on the west side of the Blackburn place. We sat still, searching as far as the lights could penetrate, but there wasn't a cow to be seen—only stars, and if you looked long enough, the silhouettes of trees way off in the distance, on the far side of the field.

Daddy turned off the engine and reached into the glove compartment for the flashlight. "Come on," he said.

We stood by the gate and listened, but all we could hear was a whippoorwill and something small rooting around in the bushes, probably an armadillo or a raccoon, as he shone the light around. He walked back to the truck, reached into the cab, and took his shotgun from the rack in the back window. He meant to sprinkle them this time, and I couldn't blame him. I was surprised he hadn't done it sooner. Buckshot wouldn't hurt them much at a distance, their hides were as tough as tractor tires anyway, and it might just convince them once and for all to find something else to eat or another field to eat it in.

We made our way along the fence line, the air damp and heavy like before a rain, but the closest thing to a cloud was the Milky Way stretching above us like gauze. I brushed off mosquitoes, wishing I'd worn more than a T-shirt and cutoffs. After a quarter of a mile or more, we reached the ridge. Daddy stopped, spit tobacco, and scratched the back of his neck, which made the light flicker over the soybeans and the trees across the fence.

Suddenly he tensed like a setter on a covey of quail and cupped his hand to his ear. He raised his finger to his lips and slowly nodded at me. I could hear the tinkling of a cow bell, not too far on the other side of the ridge. We eased down the slope and before long, about thirty feet in front of us, Daddy leveled the light on the bull and six cows, the beans flattened all around them. There was one less cow than before, and I wondered if it had gotten down and maybe the coyotes got her. They were hell on babies or anything sick or lame.

They looked at us like you would watch a boring rerun, their eyes softly gleaming in the light as they chewed. Any other smart animal would have been afraid, but not them. They went right on pulling up clumps of beans and eating them like we weren't even there.

"They sure ain't skinny anymore," I said. Daddy just grunted, so I clammed up.

"Here, hold this." He plunked the flashlight in my hand and brought the gun to his shoulder.

Dread gripped me tight around the middle. "Hey!" I said, my voice as shrill as a girl's, "You're way too close to sprinkle them!"

"Hold the light still!" he said, taking aim at the bull. The cows stopped eating, staring at us with apprehension, and they began to huddle closer together and back up to the fence. "I said hold the goddamn light steady, Jeff!"

My heart felt like a wild mustang kicking in my chest, and I tried to say something, but nothing would come out. The sound of gunshot tore through the air, ricocheted off the sky, and crashed down around my ears. The bull bellowed as his front legs crumpled, and he fell to the earth with a thud. I stood there unable to move, not believing what I was seeing. The bull exhaled one last time then grew still, his half-closed eyes staring at the darkness. I felt sick with the realization that Daddy had put slugs in the gun, not buckshot, and that he had planned to kill them all along.

The gun went off again, and another cow fell close to the bull. With fear in their eyes, the others backed against the fence as far as they could, moaning low, too confused and frightened to know what to do. Daddy moved in closer, and my brain scrambled to make sense of it, but it just couldn't. My mind was blank—I couldn't have told you my name was Jeff Arnold, or that I lived in the state of Alabama. All I knew was that the gun was firing, and the cows were bawling and collapsing and falling in the humid, suffocating air.

Not even a whippoorwill broke the silence that followed. The cows lay before us, as if they were sleeping, only their heads were at weird angles and their eyes were open. I couldn't stop staring at them lying there with the stars above them, hunger their only crime. Daddy dropped the gun to his side, breathing like he'd just shoveled a truckload of dirt, looked at them a few seconds and started back up the ridge. After a few steps, he turned around. "You coming?"

When we got back to the truck, he took a long drink of whiskey, then we rode a long time without talking, listening to the seat springs creaking and the hood clanking every time we hit a bump. But then he started talking about how happy he was that I was going to play football again this year and that he had been so proud when Coach Thompson told him I was the best player he'd seen in years. I rested my head against the back of the seat and looked out at the night.

"You okay?" he asked.

"Yeah. Just tired, that's all."

I felt him staring at me, but then he reached over and turned on the radio, to the classic country station out of Dothan. "The Way I Am," his all time favorite Haggard song, was playing, and he turned it up. I'd never heard that song without picturing Daddy on a blue bayou with a fishing pole in the sand, like the lyrics said. I'd always liked imagining him that way, instead of the way he usually was: worried, trying to piece together an old tractor or replace a worn out plow. But I didn't picture him that way then, and I doubted I ever would again.

When we got home, he and Francine went into the living room, but I said goodnight and went straight to bed. For hours I lay listening to an owl across the road, thinking about my mama. Now that I was sixteen, it didn't make me cry the way it used to. Now it made me feel better, like when you've got a fever and somebody wipes your face with a cold cloth.

Somewhere on the edge of a dream, I saw her. She was walking down a sandy lane, as graceful as a willow in the breeze, with the cows trailing behind her. The path led to a pasture—the lushest, greenest one I'd ever imagined—beneath a sky splashed bright pink and gold. Smiling, she looked back at them, and they lowed happily, following her to that beautiful place.

EASTER

Danny's mother enters the room with a basket on one arm and a two-liter bottle of orange soda cradled in the other. In the basket are two pale turquoise eggs, some Hershey's Kisses, and her old cell phone, lying on plastic grass. She sets both items on the nightstand and bends to kiss his forehead. "I'm sorry I didn't make it by last Friday," she says, "but Arthur was killing me." "Arthur" is what she calls her arthritis.

He turns his attention back to the TV mounted high on the wall and watches the contestants on *The Price is Right* as they try to guess the cost of a hot tub. "Thirty-two hundred," Danny says.

"The actual retail price," Drew Carey announces, "is three thousand five hundred and ninety-nine dollars."

A chubby, dark-haired woman looks at him wide-eyed, then claps her hand over her mouth and runs up some steps to join him.

His mother pats his cheek. "Well, you were close."

"A lot closer than she was."

She walks to the window, pushes back the heavy blue curtains, and opens the blinds.

Danny squints at the sunlight. "Geez, Mama, do you have to do that every time?"

"You need some light in here. There ain't no sense in you lying holed up in this room like a mole." She drags over a chair and sits down. "Have they got you up today?"

He shakes his head. It should be obvious that they haven't. He's still in his pajamas. Many days they don't get him up at all, but his mother likes to think otherwise, so he lets her. "Would you pour me a little water please?" His mouth feels like he has been eating glue.

She holds the mint-colored container awkwardly with her twisted fingers, and pours a cup. Balancing it between his wrists, he drinks, then lowers his head to the pillow again. On the TV, the girl squirms, wringing her hands as she tries to guess the price of a bedroom suite. She's so far off it irritates him.

Out in the hallway, doors slam and people cry out and rubber-soled shoes squeak on linoleum.

His mother smooths her hair with the back of her forearm and winks at him. "Hey, I've got some news," she says.

The girl looks as if she might cry, and Drew puts his arm around her, telling her that her guess was a good one, though apparently it wasn't. A commercial comes on.

"Well?" his mother says.

"Well what?"

"Well, don't you want to hear it?"

"Hear what?"

She frowns. "The news, Danny Lee. Don't you want to hear the news?"

No, he doesn't. Not in the least. He doesn't have much patience for her endless, pointless stories about the gaggle of old women she hangs around with, like the one who sees the face of Jesus in tree trunks or the one who only wears yellow. But he sighs and turns to look at her. "All right. What is it? What's the news?"

She leans close, peering into his eyes. "I got a phone call last night."

Her voice is barely above a whisper, like she's divulging the whereabouts of the holy grail. Noticing the peculiar way the wrinkles make swirling patterns around her mouth, he thinks how sad it is that she's grown old so fast. Life has been anything but a picnic for her, what with taking care of him and then his daddy dying. He sighs and looks up at the TV again. One of his favorite commercials is on. He likes the way the little boy talks with a lisp. It reminds him of a kid he knew in fourth grade who used to eat crayons.

"Danny, I'm trying to tell you something," says his mother.

"Okay. Would you please just go ahead and tell me who called you last night?"

With a sly smile, she leans back in the chair. "Guess."

He rolls his eyes. "God, I don't know, Mama. Elvis?"

"Danny Lee," she chides.

"Well, who then... Charlotte?" Charlotte is her sister who lives in Birmingham with her dumbass husband who used to fill gumball machines for a living.

"Now, you know Charlotte calls me all the time. That wouldn't be news, now would it?" She drops her hands to her lap, exasperated. "You're not even trying."

He knows she's trying to be playful, that she just wants to cheer him up like always, no matter how bad she feels, so he forces a smile. He thinks of the man she dated, or as she put it, "spent time with" the last year Danny was home. "Old man Merrick?"

"Lord, Danny, Fred Merrick's been dead a year now."

That was news to him. She'd probably told him, but he didn't remember. He figured they'd just stopped seeing each other. Well, dead would explain it. "I give up then."

She crosses her legs, propping her arms on her stomach. "Janine," she says. "It was Janine Carter."

He stares at her for a long moment as the name rings through his head like church bells. No other name ever sounded as good—even now.

Closing his eyes he sees her: Miss John J. Ward High School, perched on a white crepe-papered float, wearing the blue dress her mama took her to buy in Mobile. She's waving and smiling and bending to scoop candy from a plastic bucket with a gloved hand as the parade makes its way down Main. And right behind her, in the back of Coach Lowry's pickup, he stands with the other football players. All around him, they're jostling and punching each other, but he can't be bothered. He's too busy watching her. Janine is the girl he's going to marry. They're already secretly engaged.

His mother's phone rings loud enough to wake the dead, and with effort she removes it from the basket. "Oh, hey, Ruth."

He can't believe it. Janine Carter, after all this time. Why was she calling? What could she possibly want? He is impatient for his mother to get off the phone. He wants to hear everything.

After what seems like an eternity, his mama tells her friend that she'll be ready in an hour and hangs up.

"Well?" he says.

"Oh that was Ruth wanting to know if I need anything from Walmart."

"No, Mama, I mean Janine. What else did she say? What did she want?"

"Well, she said she thought you were still at home. I guess nobody ever told her any different." She frowns and looks down at her hands. It makes her sad that he's not home anymore, even though he's told her a thousand times that she's not able to take care of him any longer.

"And?"

"She wanted to know if she could come see you."

He studies a brown water stain on one of the ceiling tiles, a stain that was there before they replaced the roof last summer. It looks like a plus sign or maybe a cross. "She's here visiting her folks then?"

"The way I understood it, she divorced and moved back here, but she didn't say how long she's been here or nothing like that, and I didn't ask. I didn't want to pry, you know. She said she was working out at the paper mill as a secretary... or maybe a receptionist. I can't remember."

He clears his throat and makes himself wait a few seconds before asking, "Did she say anything else?"

"We just chatted, you know. Small talk. I asked about her folks. I heard that her daddy had bypass surgery a while back. And let's see... she mentioned those two boys, said they're teenagers now." She pours more water into his cup and takes a sip. "Mainly, she just wanted to know if it would be okay if she came out here. I told her you were awfully particular about that, but she wanted me to ask you anyway and let her know. I didn't want to flat out tell her she couldn't and hurt her feelings. I always thought a lot of that girl."

He pushes the button to raise his bed so that he can more easily see out of the window. Outside, a bluebird is perched on a feeder, turning its head from side to side. For a minute the possibility of it beckons, the possibility of seeing her again, but just as quickly reality sets in, the way it always does—in the morning when he leaves off dreaming, at night when he wakes in the darkness, and so many times in between, and he knows that it won't ever do. Janine wouldn't even recognize him now, a TV-and valium-addicted skeleton with a life expectancy of forty-three years—six years to go if he's unlucky—doing time in an old folks' prison. It would be too depressing for them both, and besides, after all these years, why does she want to see him now? Maybe she thinks he's grown wise in his confinement, turned into some kind of guru who can help put her life back on track, or maybe she's just feeling sentimental and wants to stroll down memory lane.

He rubs an eye with the heel of his hand. "Did she say she'd call back?"

"Yes, after I had a chance to talk to you."

He mashes the big forward button on the remote and begins skipping through channels, unaware of what is on the screen. "Well," he says finally, "you can tell her no. You can tell her that I appreciate the thought, but no."

His mother adjusts herself in the chair, and he can tell by the look on her face that she's about to start in. "I knew that's what you'd say, Danny Lee, but, son, why don't you let her come by? I don't think it would hurt a thing in this world, do you, and it might even do you some good. You know, you never see anybody except for me and the aides and nurses, and that don't count." She sighs. "I realize you don't like dredging up the past, but after all this time... well, maybe it wouldn't be such a bad thing."

He doesn't want to get into it. He shouldn't have to. His own mother should understand without having it explained. After all, she was there through the whole thing. "No," he says sternly. "I don't want her seeing me like this. I don't want her coming to this... this place."

She scratches a tiny bleached spot on the knee of her knit pants, as if that will make it disappear. "All right then. If that's the way you want it."

Right away, he's sorry he sounded harsh. She only wants him to have a little happiness. Not since he came to Magnolia Trace over a year ago have any of his friends been to see him—not once. Of course, most of them had stopped coming years before, except for an occasional visit on the way home from work when they'd run in for ten minutes and say, "So how are you, man?" over and over, as if he couldn't carry on an intelligent conversation anymore. Or sometimes, after they'd been hunting and were liquored up and sentimental, at which times they'd laugh about the old days and then tear up and finally shuffle out the door with their ball caps in their hands, as if they were at a funeral.

So many times he had wished they would come by and pick him up when they went fishing or riding around, the way they did the first couple of years after the accident, but he knew they didn't like the guilt they felt, and he also knew that he was a burden. It slowed them down, having to load him and his wheelchair in and out of a truck and push him around when he got out, which wasn't easy, especially on gravel or dirt. So instead he watched TV all summer long, summer after summer, imagining them camping on the river or pulling bream from Lake Jernigan or barbequing in each other's backyards. He watched TV through every fall and winter, too, while they hunted quail and deer, envisioning their breath frosting the air and the leaves crunching under their boots.

Wincing, his mama stands, supporting herself on the arm of the chair. "How about let's go and sit out on the porch for a while?"

He shakes his head. "I don't really feel like it today." A man on a lawnmower rides past the window, momentarily drowning the noise in the hallway.

"Oh, come on. It'll do you good. You ought to see the buttercups all along the walkway. King Alfreds. And they're really showing off this year." She pats his leg. "I'll go find one of the girls to help me get you up."

He knows she worries when he stays in bed so long, so he nods. "Okay then. I guess it won't hurt to go out for a while."

An hour later, he is sitting on the porch—a big, concrete, Southern-plantation-style porch with high-backed rockers lined up along the length of it. He is alone, except for a woman strapped in a geri chair a few feet away, sleeping, her head drooped over her chest. Ruth had finished early at the hairdresser's and picked up his mother.

He hasn't been outside in several months because of the cold, and he is glad he came out. He definitely prefers the porch to the recreation room where it's always noisy and crowded with drooling old people. Most of them don't know where they are, and the ones who do just stare at him with pity in their eyes. He'd rather die than sit in there.

The woman in the geri chair stirs and blinks at him, then closes her eyes again. He hasn't seen her before, but that doesn't mean much. Except for the aides, he rarely sees anyone. Jesus Christ could be living here for all he knows.

A squirrel runs across the grass and chases another up a tree, barking. Mockingbirds swoop, and a breeze, bearing the lemony scent of magnolia, ruffles his hair. He can't believe Janine hasn't completely forgotten him. He was sure he never crossed her mind, not after all these years. What a surprise that she called. It makes him glad and sad all at the same time, a tangle of emotions he knows from experience that he will never sort out.

Memories surface and lie softly in his mind. Even now he can picture her so vividly. He recalls exactly how it felt to hold her, to smell her hair, to taste her mouth—how passion burned away everything but her.

They were to be married in a month when the accident happened. They'd finalized their wedding plans. They had put down a deposit on a rental house; they had even named their first child, though they planned to wait at least a couple of years to have a baby, after they'd saved some money. They imagined it would be a boy. Caleb, he remembers—Caleb was the name they chose. They had so many plans and such a great life ahead of them... or so they thought. He's thankful he didn't know that not one of those plans would materialize.

He remembers the day that life as he knew it ended. He had just left her parents' house. She had been going on about a china pattern, knowing full well he didn't care about things like that, and she had pouted in the way that made his knees buckle. "Do you *always* have to be such a guy?" she said.

He had pulled her close and kissed her for a long time, before noticing the kitchen clock. "Man, I've got to get going! I'll be late for work!"

The job at the paper mill was a good one, one that Janine's daddy, who was a honcho out there, helped him get, and he didn't want to make a bad impression. He had been there only two weeks, besides. He kissed her quickly on the forehead, then sprinted down the steps and out to his old Corvette. In the rearview mirror, he could see her leaning against a porch post, waving. When he knew he was out of sight, he gunned it.

He never once considered that it had just rained, and water might have ponded on the blacktop. The only thing on his mind was getting to the paper mill. But three miles down the road, on the curve just before Nelson's Bridge, he hit a stretch of standing water, and before he knew it, the car hydroplaned and began to fishtail. Desperately, he tried to steer, but the wheel turned in his hands like it wasn't even connected. He slammed on the brakes, but the car kept sliding. The tires had lost contact with the road, floating on a layer of water.

He'd heard it before, how things slow down when you're close to dying, and it was true. As the car spun, time wound down, and every one of his senses sprang to life in a way he'd never imagined possible. On either side of the road, the trees were so green they looked like the backdrop of an old-timey movie, drawn in and almost cartoonish, and the whining of the engine reverberated in his ears, clear yet somehow distant. The smell of asphalt burned his nose.

His life didn't flash before him the way people said, calling up scenes of wrongdoing or maybe things he'd done right. He felt peaceful. He calmly considered how inconvenient it would be to have the dents knocked out of his car and how much it was going to cost, in addition to the new tires he'd been needing. It was the last thing he wanted to deal with, with a wedding coming up.

These thoughts seemed to meander through his head, though they must have been fleeting. He thought of Jinks, his old beagle, and of a red-haired girl who always gave him her carton of milk in the third grade. It never occurred to him that he could die or even be hurt beyond a scratch or a few sore muscles.

He'd been in a crash before, and there was nothing to it. He and three of his friends were on their way home from a ball game, when his friend swerved to miss a raccoon and hit a persimmon tree. Except for a few branches under the car and a small dent in the fender, everything was fine, and they'd rolled out laughing so hard they couldn't get their breath.

But this time the car was spinning for what seemed like forever, and he grew impatient for it to stop. He wanted to get on with whatever he had to do to fix it. But then, he grew dizzy and started to vomit. And as quickly as a light turning off, it was finished.

A magnolia fractures the sunlight, a single ray piercing his eyes. He watches an ambulance stop at the guard shack, then he closes his eyes again and thinks back to when it ended with Janine. It's an old, old rerun he knows by heart.

It was at his parents' house, three days after Christmas. She was always there, every single day, just as she had been all those weeks in the hospital, except for when she was at work or asleep. Day after day, hour after hour, she was cheerful beyond belief, telling jokes she heard at work, bringing balloons and teddy bears and books about positive thinking. He got that hype from everybody back then—from his folks, from his doctors and the physical therapists. They told stories about paralyzed people who climbed mountains and ran marathons and did every damn other thing under the sun, leading perfectly wonderful lives.

And Janine still talked about their wedding as if he had a cold he'd soon get over. She actually seemed to believe that their plans would get back on track and chug along like before. He remembered staring at her as she talked about what color couch they should buy or what brand of washing machine was best. He couldn't fathom that she was serious. But eventually he realized that she wasn't just saying all of that, that she'd blocked out reality and truly believed in this dream of hers, this fairytale she was telling herself.

He had to put a stop to it. He would not let her sacrifice herself for a cripple. Just the thought of it was more than he could stand. All he had ever wanted faded into insignificance next to all he wanted for her. Somehow, someway, he had to make her move on, though the idea of losing her made him cry each night until he fell asleep. He even prayed to God for the strength to go through with it, to think of her and not be selfish, to let her live a normal life with a normal guy. Over time, the fear and hurt turned into anger and even hatred—anger toward a God who would deal him such a cruel hand, hatred of Corvettes and summer rains that leave water on the road—and in the end, that gave him the strength to say goodbye.

The woman in the geri chair stirs again. He looks at the blanket on his lap, the one his mama made last Christmas, or was it the one before? The years are hard to keep track of.

A familiar ache floods his heart when he thinks of how Janine left that day.

She had looked up from her magazine. "I'm sorry, Danny. I didn't hear you."

He had spoken more loudly then, over the television sounds of gunshots and galloping. "I said I want you to leave and not come back."

She blinked like he was a bright light hurting her eyes, then tilted her beautiful head, the Christmas tree lights twinkling behind her. "What on earth are you talking about?"

The shame he felt for taking so long to say it made him even madder. "I'm talking about you and me, Janine. It's over. And I don't want you coming around here anymore. Not ever."

She had smiled and walked over to his chair. "Oh, you're just grouchy. I'll go now and let you get some rest."

"I'm not tired and I don't need rest," he told her, avoiding her eyes. "I mean what I say. As a matter of fact, I'm more serious than I've ever been in my entire life. There's nothing wrong with my mind, you know."

She put her hand on his. "Please don't say things like that, Danny. It scares me."

And back and forth it went for over an hour. He hated himself for every unkind word that left his mouth, but he started it, and he knew he had to see it through, even if, more than anything in the world, he wanted to hold her and tell her he didn't mean it, that somehow they would make a life for themselves. But he couldn't believe it, and he knew that if he gave one inch, she would never leave.

Her tears wet his cheek and fell on his shirt, forming dark spots on the pale blue denim, and he was afraid he couldn't endure another minute. It took all he had in him to be strong. The agony he'd experienced all that time in the hospital, all those endless, hopeless days of trying to come to terms with what happened, didn't hold a candle to the pain he felt then... or for a long time to come.

Over the years, he had learned to give it less attention and to compartmentalize it somehow, but it had never gone away. She had called many times after that and had come by, too, but he knew the last time he watched her drive away in her Mama's Lincoln with the "Waiting for the Rapture" sticker on the bumper, that it was over.

***

He doesn't know why he agreed to it. He's taken a Valium and still he can't relax. He's back on the porch, watching cars come and go, wearing a red button-down shirt the aide picked out and helped him into. She said it looked good with his dark hair. She'd doused him with cologne, then stood back with her hand on her hip. "Sugar, you look like some kind of movie star," she said. "And I ain't joking!"

"Yeah," he answered. He's not at all sure what to make of his appearance anymore, his body has changed so much. Sometimes he gets a glimpse of the guy he used to be and thinks he still looks all right, but mostly he barely recognizes his body, so thin and elongated, like a wax figure left hanging in the sun.

His breath is even more shallow than usual as he watches cars come and go. He tells himself that this visit doesn't mean anything, not really. What does it matter what Janine or anybody else thinks of how he looks or where he lives. Maybe she won't even show.

Suddenly, he feels silly, sitting there in his hokey shirt and his jeans with perfectly ironed creases, smelling to high heaven of cheap cologne. It's obvious he's taken great pains to dress, while this is probably just one of many errands she has to run today: go to the post office, pick up milk, go see Danny.

He doesn't know what she drives, so when a blue Nissan truck pulls up, his heart skips a beat. A big man struggles to free himself from the steering wheel, then lumbers up the sidewalk, his pants legs slapping the daffodils. Minutes later, Tina, the aide who helped him dress, comes out and wakes an old woman four rocking chairs down and helps her up. Danny is glad the old lady won't be there when Janine comes, and he smiles at Tina. She winks at him as they go inside.

A white Toyota pulls into the left side of the parking lot, and even at a distance he can tell it's her. His heart pounds as he watches her walking toward him, sliding her sunglasses up over her hair. Her hair is still long, though not as blonde as it once was, and she's wearing jeans, a yellow T-shirt, and sandals. She is older, but just as pretty as ever.

Long before she reaches him, she is smiling. "Oh my God! Danny!" Laughing, she runs up the steps and hugs him, apparently not afraid she'll hurt him, which is refreshing. Her face is soft and smooth against his, and he closes his eyes for a moment, breathing in her perfume and the smell of her hair. With effort he blinks back tears.

She stands back and looks at him, her eyes watering. "God, it's just so good to see you."

"Well it's good to see you, too. Pull up a chair." He tries to sound casual, but his voice quivers, and it embarrasses him.

She drags over a rocker and sits down almost directly in front of him. Reaching over, she takes his hand and gazes into his eyes. He is surprised by yet another intimate gesture, and he looks away, at a cotton ball of a cloud suspended over the treetops. For a long moment they are silent.

"So how have you been?" she asks.

He grins. "You mean all these years or lately?"

She smiles her mesmerizing smile. "Oh, I don't know. All of it, I guess."

He doesn't know how to answer that. What could he say in a few sentences? He'd like to tell her what life has been like the past decade and a half, all the endless days and weeks and months of staring at ceilings and out of windows, of watching seasons come and go and people drift out of his life, though they continued to drive by his house every day. How could he explain the shame of a grown man being bathed by his mother or the disappointment in his parents' eyes, the parents who had him late in life after waiting so long for a child? He wishes he could describe even a small part of it, but it's a story that can't be told. And he wouldn't tell her anyway. It would only depress her.

"Oh, okay, I reckon. All things considered."

"I didn't know you were out here until I talked to your mama the other night. Nobody told me." She squeezes his hand a little. "How is it?"

He shrugs. "Ah, it's not so bad, really. All things considered."

She rocks slowly in the chair. "Well, you look good. Still as handsome as ever."

He searches her eyes for dishonesty, but they look serenely back at him. "Well thanks, Janine. Body's shot to hell." He could say that hers is still gorgeous.

She laughs. "Well... I'm waiting. Aren't you going to say I look good, too?"

"Oh, you do! Pretty as ever."

"I guess your mama told you I got a divorce?"

"Yeah, I think she mentioned it. I'm sorry to hear it."

She twists the ring on her little finger. It's silver and shaped like an infinity symbol. "Well, thanks, but don't be. He was seeing some girl at his office. So predictable it's boring, huh?"

"Well, he must be a special kind of stupid is all I can say."

They talk about her job at the paper mill, and he asks about her kids. She tells him they're adjusting to the new school, but they'll be okay. The oldest is going to play football next year, the youngest has asthma. Then out of nowhere she says, "I wrote to you, you know."

A redbird lands on the porch, hops around a few times and flies away. "I know," he tells her. He wonders if she'd be surprised to know that he still has those letters in a little box that looks like a treasure chest.

"No, I mean all the ones I never sent. I wrote tons of them, mainly when I was mad or feeling down. You know, just wishing things had turned out differently." He studies her profile and waits for her to continue. "I wanted to see you so many times, but everybody said it would be best if I left you alone, that it would only make things worse for you." She pushes her hair behind her ears and shakes her head. "I shouldn't have listened. I should've come anyway."

A big truck pulls to the guard shack, its brakes squealing to a stop. He looks down at his new tennis shoes. He can guess what they told her, especially what her mama told her, but he didn't blame them. It was only because they loved her and didn't want her to tangle herself up in his tragedy again.

"Ah, don't worry about that stuff," he says. "It's all over and done with. Ancient history, as they say." But he's touched to hear that she'd written the letters, even if she never mailed them.

He had written to her, too, he could tell her. Over the years, he had written to her a million times in his mind, but even if he had been able to write, he wouldn't have sent the letters either. She had her own life, and from what he imagined, a good one, and he never wanted her to feel guilty. He wouldn't have known where to send them anyway. Her mother would have thrown them away had he sent them there.

They watch the truck drive around back to the maintenance building. An old man with a walker comes onto the porch, the door slamming behind him, and Danny feels his face grow red. He wishes they were anywhere but here.

Janine stands and carefully pulls a necklace from her pocket, then dangles it in front of him. "Do you remember this?"

For a few moments he stares at the silver chain with a St. Christopher on it. He gave it to her on her eighteenth birthday, a month before they graduated from high school. Everybody wore them back then, Catholic or not. He recalls the day he bought it at the little shop by the bus station, the one that smelled like strawberry incense and sold bongs and beaded curtains. When he'd given it to her, she'd acted like it was the Hope Diamond, and he'd promised himself right then and there that he would try his level best to give her anything she ever wanted. He had already started putting back money for a nice engagement ring.

He swallows the lump in his throat. "Yes, I remember. Sure I do."

Before he can protest, she puts it around his neck and fastens it. "I want you to have it," she says. She looks at her watch and her eyes widen. "Oh gosh, I had no idea it was this late! I promised Mama I'd help her decorate the church for Easter. You know her, she's always doing something at that church. I swear, she's there every time they open the doors." Leaning over, she kisses his forehead. "I'm sorry, Danny, but I've got to run."

Alarmed by the abruptness of her departure, he tries to think of something to say, something profound that she will think about later, but all he can manage is "Don't wait so long to come see me next time."

She runs down the two big steps and smiles back at him. "Oh, I won't. I'll see you again before long." Halfway down the sidewalk, she pauses. "Hey, maybe I'll come by next Sunday and bring you some eggs or something."

"Oh, you don't have to do that," he answers, though she's probably too far away to hear. She opens the car door, and before she gets in, she waves, just like she's in a parade.

***

His mother fidgets with the things on his night stand: Mylanta, deodorant, ointment, cinnamon candy. "You sure are quiet today," she says.

He supposes he is. Easter was almost a week ago, and he had waited most of the morning and all afternoon on the porch, dressed again in his ironed jeans and this time an old Bob Seger T-shirt, hoping he looked a little less dorky. He had waited there until the sun was setting, and people were being herded to the cafeteria for supper, but Janine never showed. The kitchen brought his supper, too: roast beef, mashed potatoes, carrots, and a chocolate-covered marshmallow rabbit. He didn't touch any of it.

He can't think of anything but her. She is all he's thought about since the day she was here. Last night, he dreamed they were lying on a blanket at Kennedy Bridge, and she was looking for Venus. He tried to help her find it, but it was nowhere to be seen. "You know," she told him, "a lot of people think Venus is just another star, but it's so much more than that."

His mama folds a throw and drapes it over the arm of his wheelchair. "I imagine she's working a lot, Danny Lee. And with two boys and a job... well, you know she's got her hands full."

"It's no big deal."

"That's right, son. And besides, she'll be back. Just because she didn't make it by on Easter don't mean a thing." Leaning over, she straightens his pajama collar. He knows she's worried. "Hey, did I tell you that Mitzy Creel fell down her back porch steps last week and broke her hip?"

"I think you did," he says, knowing she didn't. He wishes she would go now.

Cartoon music fills the room. It's one of those old-timey Mickey Mouse cartoons, the ones he's always hated, where Mickey's legs are rubbery, and his eyes are as big as his head.

"Hmmm. I didn't think I told you about that, but Lord knows I forget what I say from one minute to the next. Anyhow, they put one of those steel plates in, you know, and I heard she's not doing good at all. I'm going to see her as soon as I can, maybe tomorrow if Ruth can take me. That Ruth... I don't know what I'd do without her."

Suddenly the door flies open, banging against the wall, and an old man in striped pajamas shuffles in. When he sees Danny, he smiles as if he's just had the biggest and best surprise of his life. "Oh Lord!" he exclaims. "I've been looking everywhere for you!"

His mother takes him by the elbow and tries to lead him to the door. "Sir, you're in the wrong room. This is Danny Morgan's room." She looks at Danny and shakes her head. "Poor thing. I'll go find somebody to get him."

"Crazy as a betsy bug," Danny mumbles.

The man stands by the bed, staring down at him and grinning from ear to ear. The sun is streaming through the window behind him, creating a bright aura around his face. White hair fringes his otherwise bald head, and his eyes are the silvery-blue of Danny's father's old Bonneville. To his horror, Danny begins to cry. Surprised, the man leans over him and tries to touch his face, but Danny turns away.

Just then, his mother returns with an aide, who puts her arms around the man's shoulders and leads him from the room. His mother closes the door, then lowers the bed and sits beside Danny on the mattress. "Don't cry, son," she whispers, wiping his tears with her misshapen fingers.

Then, with more strength than he would have thought possible, she lifts his upper body and holds him in her arms.

THE COLDEST CHRISTMAS

It's close to dark when Justin Travers pulls into his front yard and turns off his truck. Next door and down the street, houses are dripping with lights, some with inflatable snowmen or Grinches standing straight or sideways in the yard. He lights a cigarette, tosses the matches onto the dashboard, and stares at the tree in his living room window. Its lights, the only ones on in the house, look dim, like they're one step away from calling it quits. They're the big old-fashioned kind that don't do anything: they don't blink, they don't light up the room, and they hang too heavily to suit him. But they're the ones Rhonda Lyn and Megan wanted as the three of them stood in the garden section of Walmart two years ago, surrounded by artificial trees and snoring Santas.

"But Jus, these look more like Christmas," Rhonda Lyn said, frowning at the ones he picked out, the little white blinking kind.

"Yeah, Daddy," Megan said. "Those are boring." She always sided with her mother when it came to anything for the house, so he had obediently set them back on the stack of other little white blinking lights, because there was no use arguing. He couldn't win. Besides, decorating the tree was their thing, so he'd let them do it. He was content to watch them hang ornaments and throw icicles while he sipped eggnog and Southern Comfort in his recliner. Every year he looked forward to it. But not this year and not ever again.

Even with its dull lights, the tree doesn't look that bad from where he's sitting, but he knows that up close it's plain that he decorated it. The ornaments are mostly on one side, the side facing the living room, and the star is leaning toward the window, as if it might jump. It's a scraggly tree, one he bought two nights before from the Firefighters' Association on the lot by the courthouse. With Christmas just four days away, there were only a dozen or so left, and they were not the cream of the crop, with their crooked limbs and dry needles.

Tommy Dubose, a guy he had known all his life and played high school football with, carried it out to the truck for him. "Supposed to be single digits by Christmas night," he said. "They're expecting snow up in Montgomery, and we might even get some, too."

"That right?"

"Well, that's what they say anyway. I hope we do, because the kids have never seen it." He stuffed his hands in his pockets and looked at the ground. "Rhonda Lyn, any better man?"

"Oh, you know, about the same."

Tommy shook his head. "I'm sure sorry to hear it." They stood in silence, watching the cars go up and down Main. "Well," he said finally, "I better get back to helping these dudes. Merry Christmas to you, Justin."

The truck cab is cold, but he drapes his arms over the steering wheel and stares at the tree until his eyes water, and the lights are a smear of red, blue, and green. He dreads going in there. He knows she hasn't gotten out of bed all day, except to go to the bathroom and maybe to fix a Pop-Tart or a bowl of cereal. She sleeps and watches TV and that's it.

He wants to get her something especially nice for Christmas, their first since Megan's been gone, and he has the money, because work has been good. There hasn't been enough daylight to get it all done the last few months. Normally, it's slow around this time, but not this year. There's more construction than he's ever seen, and he's had so many heating and cooling systems to install that he can barely get to all of it, not to mention the new refrigeration system at the Piggly Wiggly. He wishes their finances had been that good last year, when they had to put off replacing Megan's old phone until her birthday in April. Her mother had been upset about it, but on Christmas morning, Megan had acted like the cheap boots and perfume were all she'd ever wanted. Man, she was a good kid.

He tries to think of something Rhonda Lyn might like, but he can't come up with much. Since Megan died, she doesn't care about anything, including and most especially him. He thought of making a down payment on a car, so she wouldn't have to drive her thirteen-year-old gas-guzzling SUV anymore. "The White Beast," Megan called it. But she loved his pickup, strangely enough, even though it was always dirty and full of tools and papers. He remembers one day last spring when he dropped her off at school, her friends waiting on the curb, and she said, "My friends think you're hot, Daddy. And they like your truck." It makes him smile to think of it. He had been flattered and not a little surprised.

"They do?"

She laughed and rolled her eyes. "Yes, they seriously do."

"Well, you tell them I appreciate it. Makes me not feel so old."

He rubs the fog from the window with the sleeve of his jacket. He didn't know then how old thirty-eight could feel. He takes his thermos off the seat, gets out, and crosses the yard, his boots bogging a little in the dead grass. When he unlocks the door and turns on the light, a gust of hot air blasts him in the face. Peeling off his jacket, he slings it on the couch and goes down the hall to the thermostat. Eighty degrees. "Jesus," he mutters, turning it down.

In the kitchen, he trips over a bag of beer cans he has been meaning to take to recycling. A bologna sandwich with two bites missing is laying on the counter, next to a small glass flecked with orange juice pulp. He opens the refrigerator and scans the contents: ketchup, milk, mayonnaise, juice, chocolate-covered cherries, sandwich meat, and beer. He grabs a beer and heads to the bedroom.

Rhonda Lyn is propped on a pillow, wearing the big Tweety T-shirt she has on much of the time, her hair falling from a ponytail, staring at the TV like it's the saddest thing she's ever seen. On the nightstand is a Fred Flintstone glass and a near-empty bottle of Nyquil. He lays his wallet on the dresser and drops his change into a little glass bowl. She glances at him and then back at the TV with no change in expression. Taking a swig of beer, he walks around the bed and bends to kiss her forehead. "Hey there," he says. "How are you feeling?"

"Okay."

"Uh-huh," he mumbles, sitting on the edge. She is most certainly not that. She's nowhere close to it and hasn't been in seven months. The circles under her eyes would put Dracula to shame, and she's so skinny it scares him. He pulls off his boots, then slides over and brushes her bangs from her eyes. "Have you had anything to eat?"

"Yeah, earlier."

She means two bites of sandwich, of course. She never cooks anymore or eats anything healthy, except when he fixes something, and she won't eat much of that either. Even when her mother brings her favorite dishes, she barely touches them.

"Would you like me to go get us some chicken?"

She shakes her head and leans past him to see the screen. He just got home and he's already in her way. He stands, unbuttoning his flannel shirt, takes it off, and throws it into the plastic hamper that's spilling over inside the bathroom door. It's hard to believe she used to wait for him to take off his dirty clothes so she could wash them, or that she's the same woman who scrubbed behind the toilet with a toothbrush.

He sighs and lies down facing her, and studies her pretty profile. He's always loved the way her bottom lip protrudes slightly, making her look like she's pouting even when she's not. He caresses her hand, and she doesn't move, but when he kisses her shoulder, he can feel her grow tense.

On TV, a young girl explains that she wants to have a baby, because she needs something of her own, someone that will always love her.

"Christ," he says. "Get a doll."

Rhonda Lyn turns onto her side, away from him, and pulls the covers to her chest. He rolls onto his back and stares at the ceiling. There's no use trying to reach her anymore—it doesn't do any good, and they both end up mad. Their last fight had been the worst yet. He accused her of not even trying to get better, and she had screamed that he didn't know what it's like to lose a child, which left him dumbfounded. "What the hell do you think I am, a bystander?" he yelled. She said it was different for a mother, and that he couldn't understand that. Then she'd locked herself in the bathroom, and he had driven to The Black Horse, played George Strait on the jukebox, and drunk Wild Turkey straight, until a woman put her hand on his thigh, then he came home. He'd sat in his truck for a long time that night, thinking back on the worst day of his life.

***

When the police car came to the job site that day, he figured it was one of the painters in trouble again. Dexter Thompson, another guy he'd played football with, got out of the car, spoke to one of the carpenters, then came around to the side of the house where Justin was wiring up a unit. "Can I have a word with you, Justin?" he asked.

Justin laughed. "Have a word with me, Dexter? When did you start talking like that?"

But Dexter didn't smile.

"I'll be right back," he told his helper, thinking maybe Rhonda Lyn had been in a fender bender, or that her daddy had another spell with his heart. It never entered his mind that it could be anything worse.

Standing by the police car, Dexter put his hand on Justin's shoulder. "Lord have mercy, man," he said. "I don't know how to tell you this."

That scared him. "Tell me what, Dexter? Just go on and tell me."

"It's Megan, Jus. She's been in a wreck. A real bad one."

The days that followed were like being in a time warp or some kind of weird dimension. Days and nights went by, but he had no idea how many. There were funeral directors and white caskets and people constantly hugging him and saying kind things, most of them crying. He knew them all, yet they seemed like movie characters, and none of what they said took hold in his mind. There was food he didn't touch and pills the doctor gave him, and his mother-in-law staying over. It was as if he had stumbled into a dark, deep canyon and couldn't find his way out. Yet somehow through it all, Rhonda Lyn was a beacon. He wanted to be near her, to dry her eyes and make sure she knew that he was right there. But she was lost, too, and over time she wandered so far away, he couldn't reach her anymore.

***

Christmas Eve morning, he wakes up in his recliner surrounded by beer cans, still dressed in the jeans and T-shirt he had on the night before. He squeezes his eyes shut, then opens them again, squinting at the light above him until it comes into focus: a ring of gray flowers painted on a clear globe. With an aching head, he looks at the empty cans on the coffee table and wonders if there are more in the kitchen. The Christmas tree stand is bone-dry and circled with dead pine needles that he's been meaning to vacuum. The only thing under the tree is a red sweater that he bought for Rhonda Lyn at Walmart, when he went to get more beer. The lights are on but hardly visible in the sunlight that's pouring through the blinds. He stands, nearly losing his balance.

Rhonda Lyn isn't in their bedroom or the bathroom either, so he walks to Megan's room and softly opens the door. She is asleep on the bed, with her face against a stuffed giraffe. For a long time after Megan died, she slept there, and he had been so glad when she finally came back to their room. The room is frigid, and he bends to open the vent, then takes a blanket from the chair and spreads it over her.

Pushing back his hair with his hands, he gazes around the room. He has been there only three times since the funeral: to close the vent, to look for a book Megan wanted him to read, and now. There's the picture over the white wicker headboard, of two angels kissing, and the toy box he built when she was three, next to the chest of drawers that was his as a boy. Stuffed animals, everything from a dolphin to a pig, are heaped on the bed around Rhonda Lyn. Megan's pom-poms and her favorite books are on shelves near the window, and there's a picture of him and her on her bulletin board. They're at the fair, and she's holding a stuffed panda that he won for her, now on the pile with the rest of her collection.

Rhonda Lyn's eyes move under their lids, and he wonders what she's dreaming. He hopes it's something good. He likes to watch her sleep, because she looks more like herself then, without the pain in her eyes. Quietly, he closes the door behind him and goes into the bathroom, where he swallows four aspirin, then he heads back to his recliner and turns on a western. He can't recall ever watching TV on Christmas Eve or Christmas. Megan always kept the music playing, everything from Elvis to Tom Petty, and on Christmas morning, Rhonda Lyn would sit on the floor beside him, and they'd drink hot chocolate while Megan opened her presents.

They had watched her grow from a giggling baby into a beautiful fifteen-year-old with lots of friends—a girl who made the honor roll every time, never met an animal she didn't love, and wanted to be a veterinarian some day. He looks at the pictures beside him on the end table. There's one of her in the seventh grade, wearing her cheerleading uniform, and next to it is one of him and her mother at their senior prom, Rhonda Lyn's hair down to her waist. There's also a picture of the three of them on the beach in Pensacola, with clear blue waves behind them. They look so happy in all of them, smiling as if they'd won the lottery... and they had.

He goes for a beer and when he turns around, Rhonda Lyn is standing like a ghost in front of the stove, startling him so much he spills it. "I didn't know you were up," he says, tearing paper towels from a roll. "Did I wake you?"

She shakes her head. "No. I just woke up, that's all."

"Are you hungry?"

"No." She glances around the kitchen, then turns and walks to the living room where she stops in front of the tree, looking down at the plastic bag with the sweater in it. He dries his hands on the front of his jeans and picks it up, holding it out to her.

"It's not Christmas yet. Is it?"

"Well, tomorrow."

"I didn't get you anything."

"Oh, don't worry about that. Your mama will get me some socks, and that's as much as a man can ask for."

She smiles a little.

"By the way, she called last night, your mama. She wants us to come for dinner tomorrow." He knows that won't happen.

She pulls the sweater out and looks at it. "It's really nice, Jus. Thank you."

"I'm sorry I didn't wrap it, but you know how good I am at that," he says, rubbing the back of his neck. She looks around for a place to put it. "Here, I'll take it." He stuffs it back into the bag and tosses it on a chair. "Do you want to sit in here for a while?" Before she can answer, he takes her by the arm and leads her to the couch. "Come on. You lie down there and I'll go get your pillow."

"That's okay."

"Are you sure? Here," he says, handing her the remote, "watch whatever you want."

She eases herself onto the couch like an old woman, and he sits in his chair.

"Tree looks pretty crappy, huh?" he asks.

She gives him a blank look. "I'm sorry, what?"

"The tree. I said it looks pretty awful, doesn't it?"

She lies back, resting her arm on her forehead and looks at it, then her bottom lip begins to tremble and a tear drops into her hair.

"What is it, baby?" he says, walking around the coffee table to sit beside her. Covering her face with her hands, she begins to sob. "Shh," he says, stroking her hair. "It's all right."

He feels so helpless when she does that. If it was anything else under the sun, he could fix it. If she wanted to cruise around the world, he'd make it happen. If she wanted a brand new sports car, he'd get it for her if he had to steal it. He'd even die for her without too much of a show, but he can't do anything about what happened.

"Jus?" she says, when the crying subsides.

"Yes?"

"Would you take me to the cemetery tomorrow?"

His heart sinks. "Oh, Rhonda Lyn, do you think that's a good idea?"

"Please?"

He watches dust float down the rays of sunlight and sighs. Taking her out there is the last thing she needs on Christmas Day, but he tells her he will.

She touches his cheek. "Thank you."

Before long, she's going back to the bedroom.

"What do you want me to tell your mama?" he says.

"Tell her I'm tired."

A Southern Pine Electric truck passes outside, an orange ball swinging wildly from its antenna. He fishes the remote from the couch cushions and sits back down in his recliner. Near the bottom of the tree, a light goes out, a green one. "Christmas Eve," he says, picking up his beer.

***

At 10:00 on Christmas morning, the phone wakes him. It's his mother-in-law, calling to ask in a worried voice if Rhonda Lyn can be persuaded to come over. He knows that she knows better, but he reckons it's nice of her to ask anyway. She says if not they'll be by shortly with some food and gifts, unless the roads are too iced over. He tells her they're going to the cemetery. After a long pause, she says, "Do you think y'all should do that?" He tells her no, he doesn't, but that's what Rhonda Lyn wants. "Justin, it is absolutely freezing out!" A giant purple parade turtle fills the screen, its head bobbing like a cork. She wants to know if Rhonda Lyn has been up since she saw her two days ago.

"A little."

Rhonda Lyn walks into the room wearing boots, a heavy coat, gloves, a knit cap, and a scarf, and sits on the end of the couch. As soon as he can, he hangs up. "Can we go now?" she asks.

***

Within thirty minutes, they are on the road to Bethlehem Baptist Church, Rhonda Lyn cradling the pot of poinsettias her mother brought last week. It was eighteen degrees when they passed the bank, and the heat is going full blast, but the car is still chilly. He wishes he had worn gloves, even if they were dirty work gloves, the only ones he owned. "I'll be Home for Christmas" plays on the radio and he turns it off. Reaching over, he puts his hand on hers. "Merry Christmas."

"Merry Christmas. Thanks for bringing me." She rubs the door handle and looks out of the window. "I just feel closer to her out here, somehow."

"I know," he says, but he feels just the opposite. It shatters what little peace he has regained every time he sees Megan's name in granite, not fifteen feet from his grandparents. It is the hardest thing to reconcile a slab of stone to her laughing with friends or cheering at a ball game. He'd go crazy if he saw it very often, or if he let himself dwell on the image of his little girl in a box, deep in the ground.

They drive down the clay road to the church, and he shuts off the engine. The wind whines and whips around the car, rocking it from side to side, as they look out at the tombstones and the oaks beyond them raising their bare limbs to the densely clouded sky. He gets out and opens the door for her, and, holding their coats tightly around them, they make their way to the heart-shaped stone at the back of the cemetery, the poinsettias billowing in Rhonda Lyn's face. Even with heavy coats and layers, the cold is piercing, keener than he's ever known.

She sets the plant against the headstone but it blows right over, so Justin goes to find some bricks or rocks to hold it in place. When he returns, she's on her knees running her fingers over Megan's name as a few snowflakes begin to fall. He kneels, too, and puts his arm around her. "You'll freeze out here. Let's go now, okay?"

"Do you mind leaving me alone for just a few minutes?"

He sighs, gets to his feet, and follows the chain link to the other side of the graveyard.

At the edge of the woods, a buck stands motionless, watching him, his large rack held high. Justin stands as still as a statue, barely breathing, hoping he won't spook him.

He wishes so badly that Megan could see this. She would love it—the deer with the snow falling all around him.

"It's so beautiful, Daddy," she would have said.

"It sure is, honey," he whispers. "It sure is."

When he returns to the grave, Rhonda Lyn is still kneeling, the poinsettias beating against the granite heart like wings. She's shaking all over and her lips are blue.

He stretches out his hand. "Come on. Let's go home," he says. "It's way too cold out here." To his surprise, she takes it and lets him help her stand.

LAST TIME DOWN BLACKWATER

I was going through some boxes in the guest bedroom closet, getting ready for a move back to the East Coast, when I came across my grandfather's gray sweater, folded and lying on some old Annapolis uniforms my husband hadn't fit into in years. I couldn't remember the last time I'd seen it, since I stored it away fifteen years ago. It was something I'd never searched for.

I sat down cross-legged on the floor, took it out and held it in front of me. It was covered with tobacco juice stains, just like it was when my grandfather wore it over his overalls and flannel shirts, not at all like the clean, soft sweaters you associate with kindly old grandpas. But then, he wasn't a kindly old grandpa. He was gruff and loud and painfully honest, and there wasn't much of anything he could do without making a mess.

He tried my granny's patience. He ate sugar right out of the bowl, in spoonfuls. He blew his nose and wiped it on the legs of his overalls sometimes. He listened to Hee Haw and the Grand Ole Opry so loud you couldn't stand to be in the same room. And he loved to joke with people. He would ask couples with babies if they were going to try to raise them, but (for the most part) they knew he was kidding. He spit tobacco juice into a big coffee can that he kept by his orange vinyl rocker, and on long winter nights, he cut figures from newspaper flyers with his razor-sharp Case knife, making paper dolls of women in business suits and men in their underwear smiling at each other, letting them drop into the can and all around it.

I stretched the sweater out on the floor, remembering the way he wore it buttoned all the way up, or only at the top, but rarely not buttoned at all, and I could see him, a short, stout man with a round belly, walking through the back door with the smell of fall clinging to him—cold air and grasses—with quail in the pockets of his hunting vest, their striped heads slapping softly against the camouflage fabric.

Running my hand over the nubby material, I felt something in the left pocket. I pulled out a photograph and a piece of paper, which I unfolded and read. It was a grocery list with a brown circle on it, probably the result of an overfilled cup of coffee, and on the unruled piece of paper, my grandfather had written in big, crooked letters: "flour, kane sugar, two chikens, salt pork, and light bubs." The third grade was as far as he'd gotten, though he taught himself to read blueprints so he could build houses.

I had forgotten I'd kept the list. I refolded it and looked out of the window. After all those years, it seemed that no time had passed, and it still hurt to think I'd never see him again. He had been the only father I had known growing up—the only man who made time for me. I put the piece of paper back in the pocket and picked up the photograph.

It was of him and me, one my mother had taken with his beloved Polaroid, a Christmas gift from my aunt. We are posed in front of his old pickup, his arm around my shoulder and mine around his waist, and in my other hand is a string of fish. My hair is down to my waist, and I look even thinner than usual, haggard really—a look my brother dubbed my POW look. And he was right. I did, for all the world, look like one of those poor souls reaching through barbed wire in some third world country. I was twenty-three.

Grandaddy was grinning. He was in his late seventies then, but he looked older, the way people who have just found out they have cancer often do, but it also didn't help that he refused to wear his teeth, another thing my grandmother fussed about. His mouth was a dark crescent in a face that wore a rather pleading expression. He looked small and feeble, so unlike the strong, well-built man he had been. The dirty brown hat he wore everywhere, an old fedora, was pushed back on his head, revealing a few remaining tufts of white hair. On the back of the picture, I had written: August, 1983. Last time down Blackwater.

***

That summer, I had left my husband and moved back to Rock Creek, Alabama. I was living with my mother and stepfather, though I spent most nights next door with my grandparents, to help keep an eye on Granny. She had Alzheimer's and sometimes woke up and wandered. We'd found her once on the back porch at 3:00 in the morning, with a chamber pot, which we called a "slop jar," filled with Windex, talcum powder, and potatoes. When we told her brother about it, he laughed until he couldn't catch his breath.

Grandaddy didn't sleep well either. With Granny in another room, after almost sixty years of sleeping in the same bed, I'm sure he missed her beside him. Off and on, he would moan all night, though the doctor assured us that the cancer was still in the earliest stages and probably wasn't causing much pain. He liked a light on, too, so we kept on a dim one that shone from the kitchen through his bedroom door.

He was afraid of dying, and I could understand that. It was a subject that occupied my thoughts then, too. I'd started having panic attacks a few months earlier—and they terrified me. My heart raced, I felt as if I were trying to breathe with wet quilts on my chest, and my senses grew heightened. Birdsong was too shrill, and dogs barked too loudly. I became morbidly introspective, intensely focused on every heartbeat. Even with people around, I felt utterly alone, knowing beyond all doubt that no one could save me. I was convinced I was dying.

My mother was worried, and it bothered me. She didn't need that on top of everything else. She didn't know what to do when I got that frantic look in my eyes and began pacing the room like a trapped animal. "What *is* it?" she'd ask. "What is it that's scaring you?"

"It's like being on the front line in battle or something," I told her, "and you know that the next bullet is going to get you."

Sometimes when I'd walk into the room, she and my stepfather would stop talking. I overheard words like "nervous breakdown" and "mental collapse" as they tried to analyze the change in me, and to make matters worse, they apparently watched too much TV. Had I found out that my husband was gay, my stepfather wondered. Could the panic be caused by a hormone imbalance or maybe not enough magnesium? None of that was true, I informed them, not knowing what the truth was. I felt as if the world was dissolving around me, and nothing I had counted on could be counted on any longer.

I was depressed about my grandparents, too. It pained me to see Grandaddy so quiet and sad, sitting in his chair staring at the floor, and to have Granny smile at me across the table but not remember exactly who I was. And I was depressed about my marriage, of course. I was sorry I'd caused my husband to suffer. He was a good person, and he didn't deserve it.

We'd married right out of high school, but I didn't love him even then. From this side of all those years, I know that I married him because I didn't want to hurt him, and because I didn't know what else to do with my life anyway. When we were dating, he told me how it had nearly driven him to suicide when his ex-girlfriend broke up with him, and his best friend had taken me aside and solemnly asked me to please never put his friend through that again. Also, his father was an alcoholic, so his childhood had been chaotic and difficult—a brokenness I could relate to.

I was living with my grandparents back then, too, during my senior year in high school, because I couldn't get along with my stepfather. But when I turned eighteen, I knew I needed to venture out on my own and start paying my own way. My mother had been a single parent without a high school diploma, raising three kids by waiting tables or working as a maid, with so little child support you could barely call it that. I didn't want to live like that again.

I didn't seriously consider college either, though my grades were good. I didn't know the first thing about scholarships or student loans, and none of the teachers had ever brought it up. I thought college was for people with money, and the rest of us went straight to work.

After we married, we moved to Texas so my husband could work for an oil company, and I tried to make myself believe that I was as happy as the next person, even though I knew as early as when I told the judge "I do" that I'd made the biggest mistake of my life. I filled my days cooking and cleaning, decorating our apartment and reading a lot, but after four years, I couldn't pretend any longer. I'd tried antidepressants, but that didn't help. I'd tried church, too, but that didn't make me love him. Then one night, lying in the dark unable to sleep, I made up my mind to go home.

He cried when I left him. I boarded the bus, keeping back my own tears until we rounded the corner, and I could no longer see him standing at the depot, the collar of his jean jacket turned against the cold. Three years later, he was killed in a car wreck. After that, I couldn't remember the way he looked when he was happy. I could only recall the way he looked that day. And as I dropped a rose onto his casket, I blamed myself for his death.

If I hadn't left him, he wouldn't have been driving to the convenience store that night to get cigarettes. If I hadn't left him, those drunk teenagers wouldn't have crossed the four-lane and hit him head on. If I hadn't left him, if I had been the kind of person who kept her promises, he wouldn't have been crushed behind the steering wheel and pronounced dead before he reached the hospital.

I'd ended his life and ruined mine, too, before they'd even started. And going back to live with my mother and my grandparents made me feel like a failure, though Mama swore I was a big help with Granny. I didn't think so, since she did most everything anyway—bathing her and dressing her and making sure she ate. My aunt came when she could, but she lived in town, forty-five minutes away, and had a home and a husband, so she couldn't be there all the time. My two uncles came also, but they lived even farther away and still had busy jobs.

Mama did the cooking and bought groceries with the insignificant amount of food stamps my grandparents received each month, something Grandaddy had never agreed to, though they had been eligible for years. She paid their bills, too, with their meager Social Security checks, and if the money ran out, my stepfather took up the slack, buying extra groceries or even a new stove.

***

Grandaddy knocked on my bedroom door that late August morning. Peeking in, he crinkled his nose and said, "Let's go catch us some fish." He reminded me of an old elf when he did that, his chin and nose almost touching, and I chuckled. Half-asleep, I sat up and looked out at the mist. As usual, I hadn't slept much the night before. I'd been unsettled, contemplating my pulse as I lay in the dark with no moon silvering the windows and a silence so deep it was suffocating. But I pushed back the covers, got out of bed, and slipped into cutoffs, a T-shirt, and the old tennis shoes I'd cut slits into the night before, so the creek sand could wash through. Even though I was tired, I looked forward to spending the day on the water, where I hoped to get my mind off myself for a change.

Getting ready to leave for an all-day fishing trip wasn't like it used to be. Granny wasn't in the kitchen cooking eggs and grits and biscuits. In fact, the stove was unplugged because she still tried to cook if you didn't watch her. She wasn't bustling around, as excited as we were, talking about how many fish we'd catch and what a good time we'd have. Our lunch wasn't packed and sitting on the counter in a brown paper grocery sack. That morning, she was still sleeping. She would wake up in a couple of hours and from the time sleep left her eyes until it filled them again, she would repeat "I need to go home now. Ma and Pa don't know where I am, and they'll be worried."

Grandaddy and I sat at the table with nothing on it but a green checkered plastic tablecloth, a yellow box of black pepper, and our bowls of cornflakes, which we ate without talking. Then we fixed our lunch: Vienna sausages, saltine crackers, potted meat, half a loaf of bread, six cans of off-brand cola, and a gallon of water in a milk jug. We placed the cola and the water in a Styrofoam chest and covered them with the ice my stepfather had bought for us, and then we waited, listening to the wall clock ticking, until Mama's car pulled into the dirt driveway.

In no time, we gathered our things—a cage of crickets with a potato slice in it, a carton of earthworms, the tackle box and ice chest, our poles and lunch—and we climbed into Grandaddy's truck, Mama behind the wheel, my stepfather staying behind with Granny. After a few coughs of the engine, we puttered out of the backyard where he parked by the toolshed, around the side of the house, and onto the paved road.

We chugged along, the truck lurching now and then, until we passed the Florida line half a mile away, where the cracked pavement gave way to smooth, dark asphalt. A couple miles farther, we turned left onto the red clay road that led to Kennedy Bridge, and five or six miles later we were there.

The newer, sideless bridge had been erected next to the original, which had been there since way before I was born—a tall, rusty red structure made of iron railings and secured with Frankenstein-like bolts. The floor of the bridge was constructed of thick boards placed inches apart, which I used to walk over as a child, horrified that I would fall. The air smelled like it always did at Kennedy Bridge: like creosote and pine trees. I'd always loved being there early in the morning, because the creek looked so different then, mysterious in the mist, the forest stirring as if caught unawares.

Blackwater is technically a river, but we called it a creek. It turns into a river, a real one, just before it becomes the Blackwater Bay in Milton, Florida, about forty miles away. But as it winds its way through the Blackwater State Forest, it is, at most, the width of two or three telephone poles (the old-timey wooden ones), and sometimes more narrow. It's a calico stream of yellow and tea red, dotted with deep, black holes, and except in the deepest places, the water is as clear as glass, the white sand bottom plainly visible.

Mama helped us slide the heavy boat down the bank to the water, then she got back into the idling truck. "I'll see y'all at Cotton Bridge," she said.

"Make sure your mama eats something, Annette," Grandaddy told her.

She shot me a look, frustrated that he didn't seem to notice how she spent her life making sure her mother was taken care of. "I will, Daddy." With a concerned look, she said to me, "Y'all do be careful now." She hadn't been too enthused that we were going. I told her we would, and she put the truck in gear and drove off.

The mist was burning away quickly, giving way to the warming sun. It was going to be a scorcher, I could already feel it, but ever so slightly I could also sense fall in the air. As the truck noise faded, the sound of birds singing and water gurgling was all that could be heard. Grandaddy got into the boat first and sat down in the back, taking the paddle, while I pushed us from the shore, a routine that we knew well. I hopped in, glad to take my feet out of the icy water, took my place in the front, and we began to glide downstream.

Even before we rounded the first curve, things seemed like they once were. He was jolly and didn't seem worried about anything. "Hand me them crickets," he said, his voice grown gruff again, and I happily passed them to him. Propping his bare feet on the ice chest, he baited his hook. He'd already rolled the legs of his overalls to his knees.

We stopped at the first deep hole we came to, and he cast with his BreamBuster, the flexible cane pole he liked best, the red plastic bobber hitting the water with a plop. The sun was fully out now, and the day was heating up quickly. Being on the water with the sunlight flooding everything, I started to feel better than I had in months.

Right off the bat, Grandaddy caught a bluegill, so we tried that hole a little longer, but when nothing else bit, we floated to the next one. A few bends down the creek, he pointed to a dark stretch of water beneath a stand of cedars. "Do you remember the gar I caught right over there?"

I thought for a moment. I remembered the gar, but I didn't remember where he'd caught it. "Yes sir," I said.

"It was the biggest one I ever saw on this creek. Those things will sure ruin a good fishing hole."

We had been wading that day, and he had taken the gar to the bank to unhook it, showing me its needlelike teeth before throwing it back. "Don't you ever handle one of these," he admonished, as if I'd consider it. The only other fish he never let me handle were catfish, because they could fin me. Anything else, I was on my own. I had baited my own hook from the first time I picked up a pole, using crickets or earthworms or worms from Grandaddy's catalpa tree. It was important, he said, that I learn to do things for myself.

Once when we were pond fishing, I'd hooked a three-and-a-half pound bass on a cane pole, and he just watched. It wrestled and thrashed and pulled like a whale, and I begged him to help me, but he wouldn't. Finally, I'd trudged up the bank, the pole slung over my shoulder, and dragged it to the shore. On the way home, he had stopped to show his neighbor, who lived half a mile from him, and bragged, "She caught it on a cane pole. All by herself."

As we drifted along, Grandaddy would occasionally point and say, "Your Uncle Joe caught a fine trout just the other side of that sandbar the summer he got back from Korea," or "Your daddy caught the biggest goggle-eye I ever saw come off this creek, right over there by that log." Daddy was a subject I didn't know much about, since he'd left when I was six, but I liked hearing "your Daddy." It made him seem more real to me, in a way.

The morning passed quickly as we chatted and cast and pulled fish into the boat, Grandaddy assessing each one. "Oh, that's a nice one," he'd say, or "This one's a little small, but your mama likes them best, so maybe we'll keep just a few." He caught a jackfish and threw him back. I reminded him of one we kept once that he cut into chunks and Granny fried golden brown. "Yeah," he said, "they have a good flavor, but they're just so bony."

By lunchtime, we'd caught twenty-one: bluegills, redbellies, goggle-eyes, and two small trout. He nodded at a big sandbar. "Let's stop over there and eat us a bite."

That sounded good to me. I was hungry, something I rarely was anymore. I splashed into the cold waist-high water and pulled the boat to shore, then he handed me the lunch sack and stood with effort, rubbing his knees. Carefully, he climbed out, sat, and stretched his legs on the sand, his feet wide apart like a child's.

I ate a potted meat sandwich so fast I almost didn't taste it and started on another while he ate slowly, with the air of a man who has learned that it's not so important to rush, although it was probably just lack of appetite. He didn't eat much anymore, and you could tell it by the way his overalls hung in folds.

As we ate, he told the story I'd heard many times, of how he met Granny. It was after his mother and stepfather made him and his oldest brother leave home, having decided that thirteen- and fourteen-year-old boys were old enough to make their own way. They found someone to give them work and a place to live, and that someone happened to be Granny's uncle.

I'd heard the story many times, but the injustice of it still annoyed me. I was bewildered that he could so easily forgive his mother, but there was no need to tell him that. He'd only say, "I don't hold it against her. She didn't know any better." She picked cotton for fifty cents a day, he would tell me, and she couldn't read or write her name. I remembered her, though I'd seen her only a handful of times: a scowling, snuff-dipping old woman in a bonnet, who wore long dresses and brogans, and didn't like girls. I used to think it was good enough for her that she ended up the way she did, in a nursing home in Opp, Alabama, where Grandaddy was from.

He sat his Viennas on the paper sack beside him, having eaten only two. "Your granny used to love them things," he said.

"Mama can still get her to eat them sometimes, when she won't eat anything else."

It thundered in the distance, and I looked up. A purple-black cloud hung over the treetops in the west. He pulled a pouch of Red Man from the bib of his overalls, slivered the top edge with his knife, then packed the loose tobacco into his mouth, a few dark shreds dangling from his lips. "She loved sardines, too," he said. "You know, those little bitty ones." He smacked the tobacco into manageable size, then spit, moved the wad to the side of his mouth, and stopped chewing for a while.

A hawk flew over, its shadow darting across the sand, and we watched it soar straight up, then spiral gracefully down the sky, crying loudly. The sound rippled through the woods. Grandaddy folded his arms and slowly shook his head. "You know, I never dreamed she'd end up the way she has, your granny." I dug my toes into the wet sand at the water's edge and nodded.

Suddenly, his face contorted and he began to sob. I nibbled a cracker and watched a fox squirrel chase another from a holly tree. I wanted to say something to make him feel better, but I didn't know what. I didn't know why my grandmother, Sarah Elizabeth, a woman who laughed so easily and had a heart as big as the sun, had such a horrible disease. I didn't know why Grandaddy, who hadn't smoked in thirty years, had lung cancer. I didn't know why I was afraid of living, and more afraid of dying.

If I had that moment to live over again, I would go over and put my arm around him. I would tell him that I hadn't yet loved a man deeply enough or long enough to imagine how it would feel to watch him forget what we meant to each other. I would tell him that I knew it cut him to his core that Granny could recite twelve verses of a poem she learned in grade school, but couldn't remember the births of their children. "Hey, Grandaddy," I would say, "let's talk about it. Let's sit right here on this sandbar and talk about it until we find a way, somehow, to come to terms with it." But I didn't.

He rubbed his eyes with the heels of his hands, then partially rolled onto his side, pushing against the sand, and stood. He waddled to the boat, his bowed legs moving stiffly, and he rummaged around in the tackle box, but didn't take anything out of it.

He had always been a talker. He could tell stories like no one else, and he would give his opinion in a flash, but he rarely talked about his emotions. I never saw him kiss Granny until their fiftieth wedding anniversary, although I never doubted that he adored her. He didn't tell my mother that he loved her when she was growing up, something that would have made a difference in her life, I figured. He was one of those men who thought that showing you was enough. He earned a living and kept a roof over your head, and if you didn't get the idea, that was your own fault. Since he'd grown old, though, he cried sometimes, and he'd told me quite a few times that he loved me.

He picked up his pole and winked at me. "You ready to get at 'em again?"

I stood, brushing the sand from my shorts. "Are you kidding? I was born ready!"

***

When I saw it, my heart sank. A large water oak had fallen across the creek, stretching from one side to the other. It lay at a slight angle, still alive, its roots partially attached to the bank, which was about seven feet high. Grandaddy paddled to a log whose top was sticking out of the water and told me to take hold of it. I reached over, grabbed it, then tied the boat to it with the yellow nylon rope. We sat in silence, staring at what lay before us.

"Well, sugar," he said, "it looks like we're into it now."

I agreed. The boat was heavy. I didn't see how we could get it through the vast tangle of limbs and branches, and nowhere was there room to go under the trunk. He surveyed the situation, and after a little while, he removed his hat, scratched his head, and pointed to a place near the top of the tree.

"I reckon we'll have to try it there."

I hopped into the water and waded over, fighting the limbs until I reached the trunk, then I scrambled up and cautiously stood on the slick bark. "Yes sir, it looks like the best bet from here. But it sure isn't going to be fun." I twisted water from the hem of my T-shirt and looked up at the sun. It was already after 1:00, I guessed, and we were still a long way from the Cotton. Mama would be there at 5:00.

"Well, we can't sit here all day," Grandaddy said, getting to his feet.

Gripping the boat, he stepped into the water, soaking his overalls to his hips, untied it, and guided it toward me in the soft current. I jumped down and helped him navigate until the front of it hit the tree trunk. Then, taking hold of the bow—one of us on each side—we braced our feet in the sand.

"Ready?" he asked.

I nodded. On the count of three, we lifted and pulled as hard as we could, until the front of it rose out of the water, just enough to rest on the trunk, the current helping to keep it there.

Suddenly, a hacking cough doubled him over—a deep, chest-rattling cough that alarmed me—and I wondered if we should have listened to Mama. He was so frail, and his drenched overalls accentuated how thin he had become. The coughing went on for two or three minutes, but it seemed much longer. When it finally subsided, he spit dark burlap-colored mucus into the water.

"Are you okay, Grandaddy?" He just nodded, his head hanging low.

When he was breathing normally again, we hoisted and pulled some more, wood squeaking against wood, and sweat dripping from our faces. Gradually we wove the boat through, breaking branches as we could and turning the boat almost sideways at times, stopping now and then to untangle a pole, or to retrieve something that had fallen out, or to rest.

When we finally cleared the tree, we pushed the boat to the bank, where he sat, panting, his face as red as a stop sign. He unbuckled a gallus and mopped his face with it.

"Oh, look at your arms!" I said.

They were scratched and bleeding, much worse than mine. He glanced down at them and shrugged. "Skin's thin as rice paper."

The water pushed us gently onward, requiring only slight turns of the paddle to keep us on course. We drifted for a long time without talking, watching clouds ramble across the sky and water bugs swim wildly in circles near the shore. Grandaddy didn't fish at all.

"I believe I'll stop for a while, too," I said, taking the paddle. We had to hurry to make the bridge by 5:00.

We passed the old trestles, or what was left of them, a few jagged pieces of wood worn to about feet tall, sticking out of the water. A train had once hauled trees from the forest to the Bagdad Land and Lumber Company, a place that employed a lot of rural people during the Depression. Every time we'd passed them over the years, Grandaddy had told me about that, but he didn't say anything that day. Instead we quietly floated through them, and I looked back, imagining the long-ago train threading its way through the deep woods.

A cloud slid over the sun, and a breeze rippled the water. A mockingbird sang and blue jays fussed in the trees. Grandaddy took off his hat, thoughtfully pushed out the dent in the top, and put it back on.

"Do you ever wonder what it's like to die?" he said, so faintly I almost didn't hear him.

I was opening the ice chest to get our jug of water, but I stopped, sat back down, and looked into his eyes. In them I saw fear.

Of course I thought about it—almost constantly—I could tell him. But he didn't know that, and I didn't want him to. "Yes, sir," I said. "Sometimes."

He looked past me, at what lay ahead. "I just wonder what it's like, that's all."

At 5:25, the river widened, and we passed the large expanse of sandbar this side of Cotton Bridge. When we rounded the curve, there was the old truck in the distance, parked on the clearing beside the bridge. Mama sat on the ground, her arms around her knees, but when she saw us she sprang to her feet, sweeping her arms through the air as if she thought we might float past her, all the way out to the Gulf of Mexico.

***

Over a year later, after chemotherapy, radiation, and brief stays in the hospital, my grandfather, Angus Adams, left this world. On the day of his funeral, a cobalt blue-skied October afternoon, the church was filled with flowers and so many people that some had to stand outside. Granny could no longer walk, so she sat in her wheelchair next to the front pew, cheerfully singing along to "Firmly Promise Me."

After they lowered the casket into the ground beneath the old oaks, and after most of the black-clad people left food and went home, I borrowed Mama's car and drove to Kennedy Bridge. I'd been anxious all day, even frightened. During the funeral, I'd worried that I might have a full-blown panic attack.

I parked the car, walked to the old bridge, and sat with my legs dangling over the side. I thought of our last trip down the creek that August day, of the fallen tree, and the obstacles Grandaddy had faced in his life—obstacles I knew I would face as well. Sitting there, in the space between regret and new beginnings, I didn't know what I'd do. I didn't know where I'd go or how I'd get there. But I knew that I was my grandfather's granddaughter, and that somehow I would always find a way.

Beneath me, the water flowed with barely a sound, and my heart grew tranquil. All around, the pine trees swayed, murmuring a melody that I knew well, and I held my breath to hear.

Having resided in several parts of the country (and abroad), Sharon now lives in Northwest Florida with her husband and their dog, just down the road from her home state of Alabama.

www.ingramcontent.com/pod-product-compliance
Lightning Source LLC
LaVergne TN
LVHW020047110826
845155LV00029B/672

* 9 7 8 1 9 3 9 2 8 2 6 1 3 *